doubl...

LOVE BYTES

Read more about love on the Net in

Double Click Café 1: Cyber Kiss   *Marilyn Kaye*

double·click·café:2

LOVE
BYTES

marilyn kaye

Collins
An imprint of HarperCollinsPublishers

For Isabelle and Christophe Clerc,
who opened their home and their hearts,
I give you this book (and my heart) in return.

First published in Great Britain by Collins in 1997
Collins is an imprint of HarperCollins *Publishers* Ltd
77-85 Fulham Palace Road, Hammersmith, London, W6 8JB

1 3 5 7 9 8 6 4 2

Text copyright © Marilyn Kaye 1997

ISBN 0 00 675261 6

The author asserts the moral right to be
identified as the author of the work.

Printed and bound in Great Britain by
Caledonian International Book Manufacturing Ltd,
Glasgow G64

Chapter One

At one o'clock on a Monday afternoon, the cafeteria at Briarcliff High School was in its usual state of noisy chaos. Students carrying brown lunch bags or balancing trays of food, anxious to make the most of their thirty minute lunch period, hurried to meet their friends at the tables.

At one table, Jessica Porter joined two other girls from the junior class, Caryn Singer and Blair Moorhead.

'Hi, guys,' she said as she sat down. She opened her brown bag and removed a neatly wrapped tuna sandwich, a bag of cheese crackers and an apple. She glanced at the tray of food which lay practically untouched in front of the girl who sat across from her.

'Yuck, what's that?' she asked, mentally congratulating herself for having the foresight to bring her own lunch from home. Actually, she couldn't claim any special gift for predicting the future – the lunches at Briarcliff High were notoriously foul.

Across the table, the petite girl with short, straight brown hair and the unidentifiable meal didn't bother to look up. 'I don't know and I don't care.'

'Uh-oh,' Jessica murmured as she unwrapped her sandwich. 'What's up?' She knew it couldn't be the food that was putting Blair in such a bad mood.

Blair just shrugged, and continued to examine the mess on her tray. Jessica turned to the girl beside her. 'What's going on?'

Caryn sighed. 'It's Denny.'

'Oh.' She gazed at Blair, preparing to offer her friend compassion. Blair and Denny hadn't been together very long, and as of last Friday, Blair had still been high on him. 'What did he do?'

Blair finally looked up, and she spoke mournfully. 'He said he thinks we should start seeing other people. Which basically means he wants to dump me.'

Jessica didn't attempt to argue that, since Blair was probably right. Any guy who said something like that after only two weeks of dating was trying to kill a relationship before it got too heavy. So she just shook her head sympathetically, and said, 'That stinks.'

'I don't understand!' Blair moaned. 'Everything was going OK. It wasn't like I was being pushy, asking him for some major commitment or anything like that. I played it totally cool. I don't know what I did wrong.'

'Has it occurred to you that maybe you didn't do anything wrong?' Jessica suggested.

'Then why is he dumping me?'

'Because you're not meant for each other,' Jessica declared. 'He's not the right guy for you.'

'That's what I told her too,' Caryn said. 'You see, Blair? You can't think it's your fault.'

'Yes I can,' Blair responded gloomily. 'It *is* my fault. Because I always go for the wrong guys. Remember Tony Evans? And Eric Persky?'

'You can't blame yourself for falling for them,' Caryn said. 'They're both really cute.'

'Cute isn't everything,' Jessica commented. 'You shouldn't base an attraction on that. Look at Andy, for example. He's not particularly gorgeous.'

Blair seemed a little shocked. 'Jess, how can you say that? He's your boyfriend!'

Jessica grinned. 'I'm not saying he's ugly. But no one's going to give him a prize for his looks. Not with those freckles.'

'How long have you and Andy been going together?' Caryn asked her.

'Four months, one week and two days,' Jessica replied. 'It's easy to remember, because the first time we went out was on the Fourth of July, to see the fireworks in the park. And neither of us have gone out with anyone else since.'

'You're lucky,' Blair commented.

'Yeah, I guess we were lucky to find each other. It's funny, I'd seen him around school before, and we were in the same algebra class freshman year. But I'd never paid any attention to him. Freckles and red hair don't usually appeal to me. And he never noticed me because he likes petite girls, and I'm as tall as he is.'

'So if you weren't looking at each other, how did you get together?' Caryn asked.

'I ran into him at the pool last summer,' Jessica explained. 'There wasn't anyone else I knew around and I was bored, so I started talking to him. Five minutes later, I knew that we were meant to be together.'

Caryn looked sceptical. 'How could you tell?'

'Because we're so much alike! We're both very opinionated, we've both got lots of attitude, and we stand up to each other.' She laughed. 'Andy's the first guy I've ever met who I can't push around. And he knows he can't push me around either. We're a perfect match.'

Blair was looking past her. 'Here comes Mister Perfect now.'

Jessica was expecting that. Her lunch period and Andy's overlapped by five minutes. They usually spent that time bringing each other up to date on the day's plans.

Andy came over to the table, saluting them all with his friendly grin. Then he spoke to Jessica. 'Jess, you've got choir practice after school today, right?'

'No, it's been cancelled,' Jessica told him. 'Ms Robbins has a sore throat.' His face fell. 'Why?' asked Jess.

'Well, I thought you'd be busy, so I planned to go over to the Double Click after school.'

'The *what*?' Caryn asked.

Andy explained. 'The Double Click Café. It's that little snack place where you can go online, over on Clairmont Road, in the mini-mall.'

'Oh yeah,' Blair said. 'I've been meaning to check that out. What kind of Internet servers do they have?'

'Practically all of them,' Andy replied. 'America Online, Compuserve, Prodigy...'

Jessica stopped listening as Andy and Blair started speaking in computerese. She found the subject incredibly boring.

She was getting sick of hearing about the Double Click Café. Ever since Andy discovered the place two months ago, he couldn't stop talking about it, as if it had become the most exciting event in his life.

Blair and Caryn were avidly listening to his description of the newsgroups he subscribed to when Jessica broke in to the conversation. 'Do you *have* to go there today? I was sort of thinking we might go to the Mall. I want to look at stereo systems. My parents are going to get me one for Christmas and I want to tell them exactly what I want.'

'Good grief, it's not even December yet,' Andy said mildly. 'You've got plenty of time. We'll go another day.'

'And you could go to the Double Click Café another day,' Jessica retorted.

'But I haven't been there in a week,' Andy declared. 'I want to go today.'

Jessica glared at him. 'What are you turning into, a computer addict? You talk like you need a fix!' She became aware of the fact that her voice had risen, mainly because Blair and Caryn had turned away and suddenly developed a serious interest in their lunches.

Andy glared right back at her. 'There are worse things than being addicted to computers, Jess. Like having a phobia about them.'

Blair coughed politely. 'Jess, we have to get to class.'

Jessica glanced at the clock. 'Right.' She rose. 'Talk to you later,' she said to Andy.

'Yeah, I'll call you tonight,' he replied.

As the girls walked out of the cafeteria, Blair said, 'I don't get it.'

'You don't get what?' Jessica asked.

'You and Andy.'

'What about me and Andy?'

Caryn appeared to understand what Blair was talking about. 'It's a weird relationship, Jess. I mean, you guys are always fighting.'

'We weren't fighting,' Jessica stated. 'We were having a discussion.'

'It was a pretty hostile discussion, if you ask me,' Blair commented.

Jessica shrugged. 'We talk like that all the time.'

'I know,' Blair said. 'I remember that so-called discussion you two had last Friday at lunch. Over which had more nutritional value, broccoli or spinach. You guys were fighting over vegetables!'

Jessica had to laugh at the memory. 'We like to argue. What's the big deal?'

'Are you sure Andy likes to argue as much as you do?' Blair asked.

'Of course he does,' Jessica replied. 'We wouldn't stay together if he didn't. Why?'

'I don't know,' said Blair. 'It just seemed to me that he was a little ticked off, the way you were making fun of his going to the Double Click Café. He doesn't make fun of your choir practice, does he? Does he complain when you go to your ice-skating lessons?'

Jessica shrugged. 'OK, maybe I was a little rough on him. I just don't understand why he likes that place. And I wish he wouldn't hang out there so much.'

'You can't get your own way about everything,' Caryn remarked.

'I can try, can't I?'

Blair rolled her eyes. 'Anything else you want to change about him?'

Jessica considered this. 'Well, sure. I wish he could be more romantic, and pay more attention to me. Sometimes I think he takes me for granted. I wouldn't mind a compliment once in a while. Or flowers. He's never sent me flowers.'

'I don't know too many sixteen-year-old boys who send flowers to their girlfriends,' Caryn said.

'It's not really flowers I want,' Jessica said. 'It's something else. Like, just now, did you see how excited he was getting when he talked about that stupid online stuff? I wish he'd act that excited about me.'

'Maybe he would, if you weren't always picking fights with him,' Caryn said.

'I do *not* pick fights with him,' Jessica declared indignantly.

'Sure you do,' Caryn said. 'Look, I'm just saying that one of these days, Andy's going to get tired of all these so-called discussions. You might think about agreeing with him once in a while.' They had reached her classroom, and Caryn waved at the girls as she left them.

'She thinks she knows everything,' Jessica fumed.

She was surprised when Blair defended Caryn's words. 'You should think about what she said, Jess. It wouldn't hurt if you showed a little interest in what he's interested in.'

'I don't need lectures about my love life,' Jessica said, and added to herself: Especially not from someone who's never even had one.

Blair seemed to read her mind. 'Look, I know I have no business advising anyone about their relationships. But I've read enough articles in *Seventeen* and *Sassy* to know that if you don't share anything together, this relationship is not going to last.'

'So what am I supposed to do about that?' Jessica demanded. 'Fake an interest in something I couldn't care less about?'

'No,' Blair said. 'But if you want him to pay more attention to you, you need to pay more attention to him. You could try to care about something he cares about. Like, at least give it a shot. Every good relationship requires some compromise.'

They'd reached their class as the bell rang, so they had to stop speaking as they hurried to their seats. But when the bell stopped ringing, Blair's last word kept ringing in Jessica's ears. Compromise.

She *detested* that word.

* * *

When Andy walked into the Double Click Café, he felt right at home. It wasn't as if anyone called out to him or jumped up to welcome him or anything like that. It was just a feeling he got when other regulars glanced up from their screens and nodded or smiled.

He was anxious to get right online, but since he hadn't been there for a week, he wanted to spend a few minutes talking to Greg and Hilary, the young couple who owned the place. Right now, both of them were behind the newly-installed counter-bar.

The patrons had been allowed to have their snacks and drinks at the computer stations, but an abundance of crumbs and spilt coffees didn't have a very good effect on the equipment. Now there was a counter lined with stools where patrons could sit, eat and drink while taking a break from the computers.

Andy perched on one of the stools and Hilary greeted him warmly. 'Hi, stranger. We haven't seen you around here for a while.'

'I had two essays to write and a take-home exam,' Andy explained.

'You know, we've got word processing programs here,' Greg pointed out. 'You can always use our machines.'

'I didn't dare come here,' Andy told him. 'I don't trust myself. It's too easy to get out of a word processing program and into an online one.'

'What can I get you?' Hilary asked.

'Could I have a lemonade?'

'Coming right up.'

'Yo, Shaw!'

Andy turned and recognised the boy sitting at the opposite end of the bar. 'Hi, Paul. I haven't seen you around here before.'

'I just started hanging out this week. This place is cool.'

Andy nodded in agreement, amazed again at how he couldn't tell who he might run into at the Double Click. He never would have guessed he'd find Paul Reedy here. Paul wasn't a particularly good friend of his, but he knew him. Practically everybody in the eleventh grade at Briarcliff High knew Paul – he was the class clown, always fooling around and trying to get laughs. Mostly he got on people's nerves with his constant efforts to get attention and be considered cool, and the way he called people by their last names.

'What have you been doing here?' Andy asked.

'I'm checking into those romance chat lines, the ones where the cute babes hang out.'

Andy had to smile. 'How can you tell if they're cute or not?'

'I can tell,' Paul said confidently. 'I heard about this guy who met a girl online, and he fell in love before he even saw her.'

'Really,' Andy said, without much interest.

'Yeah! You ever try to meet a chick online?'

'No,' Andy said. 'I don't think my girlfriend would appreciate that.'

Hilary was setting out bowls of pretzels on the bar. 'I didn't know you had a girlfriend, Andy. How come you haven't brought her here?'

Andy smiled with a shrug, then he changed the subject. 'Have you heard about that computer virus in the Midwest?'

Greg began giving his opinion on the source of the virus, and Andy could relax, relieved that he wouldn't have to say anything more about his girlfriend. It was a little embarrassing, not to mention bewildering, the way Jessica absolutely refused to have anything to do with this place. He couldn't understand her lack of interest. He was totally captivated by the cyber world.

He finished his lemonade and left the bar, where Paul was now making dumb jokes about developing cyber-antibiotics to cure computer viruses. Greg was listening with a pained expression. Andy took a place at a computer station and logged on.

He started off by checking into his e-mail. Through various interest groups, he'd made connections with a guy in Germany and another in France, and they wrote regularly. He didn't want to call them penpals – that sounded like something a twelve-year-old girl would be involved with – but in all honesty, that's what they were.

There was a message from Dieter, a guy who he'd met in an alternative music newsgroup. It amazed him how well Dieter could write in English, even though he'd never been to the United States.

Hello, Andy. Thank you for the information about the band called Cold Medicine. I do not know this group, but I will request that my record store order the compact disc. There was a word in your message that I did not understand. What does 'ROFL' mean?

Andy composed a quick reply. *Sorry, I forgot that everyone doesn't have the same electronic shorthand. ROFL means, 'roll on the floor laughing'. Do you have special shorthand expressions in German?*

'What are ya doing?' came a voice from behind him.

It was Paul Reedy. 'Answering e-mail,' Andy told him.

'What's e-mail?'

Andy looked at him in surprise. 'Oh, come on, Paul, you have to know about e-mail.'

'Hey, man, I'm telling you, I just got into this stuff, I don't know beans.'

'Sorry,' Andy said. 'It's just that, when people get into the cyber world, e-mail is usually the first thing they learn about.'

'OK,' Paul said. 'Tell me about it.'

Andy hesitated. 'I'm not much of a teacher, Paul. There are a lot of good books you could read that will explain it to you.'

Paul groaned. 'Whoa, give me a break, Shaw, I don't want to have to wade through a whole book. Just give me the basics, OK?'

Andy stifled his own groan. He had

absolutely no desire to spend his limited time here giving instructions on electronic mail. Unless, of course, Jessica wanted to learn.

'Can you use this e-mail to meet chicks?' Paul asked.

'Stick with the chat lines,' Andy advised. 'Then, if you meet someone who wants to correspond, she'll give you her e-mail address and you can exchange messages.'

'Is that what you're doing?' Paul asked. 'Sending a message to a babe?'

Andy didn't much like those words like 'babe', or 'chick', but he didn't want to start an argument. He'd been having enough of those lately with Jessica.

'No, this is a guy in Germany,' Andy said. 'We met on a newsgroup.'

'What's a newsgroup?'

Andy tried to remain patient. 'It's a discussion group. There are thousands of them, on different subjects. You subscribe to them. Members can leave messages for each other and respond to them.'

'What do they talk about?'

'Whatever they're interested in. Here, I'll show you my newsgroups.' He clicked on Read my Newsgroups and a list of the ones he subscribed to appeared.

Paul read through the list without much interest. 'Yeah, OK.'

Andy continued to explain. 'If you're into a certain rock band, there might be a newsgroup for them. Or, or if you're into exotic fish, or video games, or motorcycles, there's probably a newsgroup. Some TV shows have their own newsgroups.'

'Oh, yeah? Like, which ones?'

Andy tried very hard to keep the annoyance out of his voice but he had a feeling he wasn't being very successful. 'Look, Paul, I've got some stuff I want to do now. How about if I show you how to subscribe to a TV newsgroup? Once you know how to do that, you can subscribe to just about anything, OK?'

'Yeah, all right.'

Andy had an uncomfortable feeling he'd just hurt the guy's feelings, but what else could he do? With any encouragement, Paul Reedy would be hanging out with him all afternoon.

He tried to think of a Television show newsgroup. 'Do you know *Nitro Man*? That's got a popular newsgroup, I've heard kids talking about it at school.'

'I never saw it,' Paul said. 'But I've heard

of it. It's weird, right?'

'I don't know, I've only seen it a couple of times,' Andy said. 'Anyway, I'll show you how to subscribe to the *Nitro Man* newsgroup. Then you can try getting into one for a show you like.'

He showed Paul the steps to accessing the newsgroups. 'You can have newsgroups searched by subjects. Or, if you know the actual name of the newsgroup, you can get to it directly.' He typed in: alt.TV.*Nitroman*. A list of topics related to the television show appeared on the screen.

'These are threads,' Andy explained. 'You can click on one and read the messages.'

'Try that one,' Paul said, pointing to a topic.

'OK,' Andy said, and he moved the cursor so he could click on *Nitro Man* as Metaphor.

The first message appeared. Since he wasn't a regular viewer, Andy didn't really get what the poster was talking about, and he couldn't imagine that Paul understood it either.

'Let's see another one,' he demanded.

Andy obliged, clicking onto next. Another long, complicated discourse about

Nitro Man appeared.

'How do you post a message?' Paul asked.

Andy showed him. 'You click on Send New Message, and a dialogue box appears for you to write it.'

Paul leant over and clicked onto Send New Message. Then he composed his message to the *Nitro Man* subscribers.

Get a life, you morons! And before Andy could stop him, he pressed 'send'.

'Paul!' Andy yelled. 'You know what you just did? You make a nasty remark like that, it's called flaming, and it's completely obnoxious! Not to mention the fact that you're sending it from *my* user name, and these people are going to think it's from me!'

'What do you care?' Paul asked. 'They don't even know you.'

'Because it's not right, that's why I care,' Andy declared hotly. 'Maybe you'd better learn something about netiquette before you get too involved with the Internet.'

'Oh, yeah, right,' Paul sneered. 'Geez, Shaw, don't you have a sense of humour?'

'This isn't funny, Paul,' Andy said. 'There are rules of behaviour you follow here, like anywhere. You'd better learn them if you want to get into this.'

'Yeah, what happens if I don't?' Paul chortled. 'They put me in cyber jail?'

He really is a jerk, Andy thought. 'Look, Paul, you do what you want. Just don't do it on my time and with my user name, OK?'

'No sweat,' Paul said easily, and ambled away to look over someone else's shoulder.

Andy quickly composed an apologetic message to the *Nitro Man* newsgroup, and then went back to his own newsgroups. For the zillionth time, he wished Jessica could get into this. He wouldn't mind teaching her everything he knew. And he could feel completely confident she wouldn't do anything as stupid as Paul just did.

But Jessica had decided this wasn't her thing, without even giving it a try. As crazy as he was about her, he did wish that just once in a while, she'd be a little more flexible.

And sometimes, he got an uncomfortable feeling that maybe this relationship wasn't all he wanted it to be.

Chapter Two

Blair's locker at school was right next to Andy Shaw's locker. Frequently, she ran into Andy there. But even when she didn't, every morning when she opened her own locker to toss in her jacket and books, her eyes strayed to his. To the upper right hand corner of his locker door, to be precise, where Andy had scrawled *AS & JP* inside a heart.

It was pretty corny, of course, but Blair thought it was kind of sweet. And he'd written it in indelible marker, which was very significant. Until the lockers were repainted – which probably wouldn't happen until the next century, if ever – those letters would be there, a permanent testimony to their everlasting love.

Blair had always admired this symbol of Andy's commitment to Jessica. But on this Tuesday morning, it depressed her too. She wondered if she'd ever find herself in a lasting relationship like theirs. Given her history with guys, always falling madly in love with the wrong type, she doubted it very much.

She closed her locker, but instead of leaving she leant against the door and observed the people who passed. Lots of them were in couples, and they strolled casually down the hallway in the usual morning promenade before the warning bell sent them scurrying to their homerooms. A cloud of despair settled on her. Would she always be walking alone?

Jessica came bounding over to her. 'Have you seen Andy?' she demanded.

'No, not since I've been here,' Blair replied.

'I think I'm going to wait for him,' Jessica declared. 'I've got something very important to tell him.'

'What?'

Jessica let out a long, melodramatic sigh. 'I'm going to tell him I'll go to that Clicky place with him.'

'The Double Click Café?'

'Yeah. I was thinking all last night. And I've decided that maybe you're right.'

Blair was startled. Jessica rarely thought that anyone who disagreed with her was right. She wasn't even sure what Jessica thought she'd been right about. 'What do you mean?'

'What you and Caryn were saying yesterday, about Andy and me. About how we fight all the time, and how I need to show some interest in what he's interested in.'

'What brought about this sudden change of heart?' Blair wanted to know.

'Oh, I just thought about what you guys said and all that,' Jessica replied airily. Then she grinned. 'And last night, I told Andy about this ice-skating show that's coming to town. You know, the show with the girl who got the silver medal at the last Olympics? And that gorgeous sexy French skater, Philippe what's-his-name? He said he'd take me to it. And I *know* he's not interested in ice skating. So I felt like I had to do something nice for him.'

Blair frowned. 'So you have an ulterior motive for agreeing to go the Double Click Café. That's not exactly admirable, Jessica.'

'Well, that's not all of it,' Jessica retorted. 'I do love him, you know, and I don't want to lose him. I figure, if I fake a little interest in his thing, I can get him to start being more romantic to me. So thanks for the advice.'

'You're welcome,' Blair replied, still not quite sure what she was being thanked for.

cally Jessica was saying that she had discovered a way to manipulate Andy – which wasn't what Blair had proposed at all.

At that moment, Andy appeared. Jessica got right to the point with him.

'Are you going to the Double Click Café after school today?' she asked.

He was a little taken aback. 'Well… I don't know, I'd like to, why?'

'I want to go with you, that's why.'

A radiant smile broke out on Andy's face. 'Great!'

'See you guys later,' Blair said, but she didn't think they heard her. They were too busy gazing lovingly into each other's eyes.

That was bizarre, she thought as she walked to her homeroom. Jessica changing her mind like that, and Andy getting so excited about her coming to the computer place… and she was sure they would now find something completely different to start arguing about. Supposedly, they loved each other, but their relationship made no sense at all.

That was the problem with romance, she decided. It wasn't *rational*. People didn't come together in a logical way. They didn't choose their mates scientifically. If they did, they wouldn't have so many problems. They'd have something in common, they'd share some interests.

Their personalities would mesh too. A quiet person who liked to read wouldn't end up with someone who wanted to go out dancing every night. A party animal wouldn't be with someone too shy to meet people.

They could have the same tastes in food, and the same taste in music. They'd have similar career ambitions, too, so they could attend the same universities, and study together. There would be no fights, no reasons to disagree. They could be truly content together, all the time.

But how could this happen? It wasn't as if you could interview someone before you went out on a date together. You couldn't say, look, I don't know if I want to go out with you, could you first answer some questions? Fill out this survey form?

At that moment, in the middle of the crowded hallway, she froze. She stopped so fast that someone behind her bumped into her. She didn't even feel it. It was as if an electric current had passed through her body.

Why not? Why couldn't you fill out a

questionnaire to determine your romantic interests?

For years and years at school, students had to take standardised tests to determine their personality type – intelligence, capability, career potential. Why not a standardised test for love? Something that would let people know what kind of person they'd be best suited to have a relationship with? And maybe even put the two people together?

She could do it. She'd always been good with computers and statistics and programming. She could work up the questionnaire, develop a means of analysing it and create a program to take the results of the analyses and match the subjects.

She was so overwhelmed by her idea, she didn't even hear the warning bell. It wasn't until the hallway was almost completely deserted that she realised what was going on. But her excitement gave her a burst of energy, and she made it into homeroom just as the final bell rang.

As Andy turned the car up Clairmont Road, he continued to explain the Double Click

Café to Jessica. He'd done this before, but this time she actually tried to listen.

'You get thirty minutes online for free, sort of a trial period. Then you set up your own account, with a password and a user name. And you pay according to how much time you spend online.'

That sounded simple enough to Jessica. Personally, however, she didn't think she'd be running up much of a bill. She didn't even know what she could find to do to fill up the free thirty minutes. But she kept her mouth firmly shut, and just murmured 'Uh-huh,' through tightened lips.

'I'll show you how to get started,' Andy went on. 'Then you'll probably want to go off on your own, and see where the links lead you.'

She tried to remember what links were. She knew he told her once, but so much of what he'd said in the past had gone in one ear and out the other. It wasn't easy trying to concentrate on his words now, it all sounded so unbelievably boring.

She was determined to act interested and not let him see what a sacrifice she was making. Right that minute, she could be at the ice-skating rink, practising her double axel. Or working on her history term paper. Or searching the mall for a pair of new winter boots. Or at home watching re-runs of *The Brady Bunch*. She could think of a million things she'd rather be doing than this.

But still, she had to admit that she took some pleasure in Andy's proud expression as he ushered her into the Double Click Café. Jessica glanced round the place. Except for the bar, she thought it looked like a computer laboratory at school.

Well, maybe not. The computer labs at school didn't have bright posters on the walls, or kids looking this contented as they worked.

'You want something to eat or drink?' Andy asked, indicating the bar.

'OK,' she said, thinking that she'd do anything to put off getting her computer instruction. As they walked across the room, several kids turned and greeted Andy.

'Hi, Andy,' said the smiling woman behind the counter.

'Hi, Hilary. I want to introduce you to Jessica.'

'Hello, Jessica. Welcome to the Double Click Café.'

'It's nice to be here,' she lied.

'Hilary and Greg own this place,' Andy told Jessica. 'They're always available to show you how to do things.'

Hilary nodded. 'But I'm sure you won't need our help, with Andy here.'

They both ordered sodas, which Hilary immediately placed in front of them. Then Greg came by and Andy introduced her. He and Andy exchanged a few words about something she didn't understand. Kids came into the café, people she'd never seen before, but they spoke to Andy familiarly and warmly.

In the back of her mind, she must have always known that Andy had a world here, a whole life she knew nothing about. But for the first time it seemed real, and she felt a little jealous.

Of course, she had a private world too that he wasn't a part of – her life at the ice-skating rink. He'd see a bit of that world when he took her to the big ice show – but that wasn't much. It occurred to her that now, since she was offering to share this world with him, maybe she could insist that he started taking ice-skating lessons with her.

The image of Andy executing a toe jump made her wince. Maybe not.

She sipped her soda very slowly, while Andy gulped his down. Obviously, he couldn't wait to get over to those computers. Well, she knew she'd have to face it sooner or later. She thought she hid her reluctance quite well as Andy led her to a computer station. She sat down in front of the computer and he pulled another chair over to sit beside her.

She couldn't remember ever seeing him so excited, as he began to describe the process of logging on. She felt like a martyr as she feigned an interest in those meaningless words which were more or less a foreign language to her. I'm giving him pleasure, she kept telling herself. I'm making him happy. That's what's important. Not to mention the fact that maybe now I'll start getting flowers.

'What would you like to dive into first?' Andy asked her. 'The Web? Newsgroups? A chat line?'

As if she cared. 'Why don't you choose for me?' she asked sweetly.

He looked at her strangely for a moment, and she knew why. She wasn't usually this willing to turn over a decision to anyone else. 'OK, we'll start with a Web page,' he said.

'OK,' Jessica echoed. 'Show me the Web page.'

'Not *the* Web page,' Andy corrected her. 'Remember, it's called the World Wide Web, and there are tons of documents all over the world that are connected.' He thought for a moment. 'You know that new Arnold Schwarzeneggar movie? The one that's set in the future where he has to wipe out an entire nation of androids infected with an evil virus?'

She shrugged. As far as she was concerned, one Arnold Schwarzeneggar movie was like any other. It was another topic of disagreement between them. 'What about it?'

'I saw a poster the other day. The movie has a Web site. I think I can remember the command. Watch.' He typed something, and hit the 'enter' key. A few seconds later, some fuzzy shapes and colours began to appear. Over the next few seconds they went into focus, and Jessica could read the words: 'Arnold Schwarzeneggar in *Total and Complete Annihilation of the Universe.*'

Total and Complete Boredom was probably more like it, Jessica thought.

'See those blue words?' Andy pointed

them out. 'Those are your links to related topics. Like, if you go here, you can see scenes from the movie. Or, if you want to know how the special effects were created, you click here. Look, I'll show you.' He began to demonstrate.

Unfortunately, Jessica soon realised that her dramatic skills were not as sophisticated or as convincing as she'd hoped they would be. Her lack of interest – no, her total and complete boredom – must have been apparent, because Andy stopped clicking.

He wasn't angry, though. 'I'm just using this as an example,' he said. 'Why don't we find a Web page on something you're interested in?'

'OK,' Jessica said. She waited.

He was waiting, too. There was a hint of impatience in his voice when he spoke. 'Well, what kind of Web page do you want to see?'

'*I* don't know,' Jessica replied.

He looked pained. 'Jess, are you sure you want to be doing this?'

'Sure I'm sure.'

He ran his fingers through his hair. 'OK, look. There's this thing called a "browser". It enables you to search the Web. You put in your topics, and the browser identifies related Web sites. I'll set it up for you, and all you have to do is enter subjects.'

He fooled around on the keyboard for a moment. 'OK, you're set. I'm going to check on my newsgroups.' He got up from the chair.

'Where are you going?' Jessica asked.

'I *told* you, I want to check on my newsgroups.'

'Can't you do that right here?'

'Jess, I can't do my thing and let you do yours on the same computer at the same time.'

I don't *have* a thing, Jessica wanted to say. I'm only here for your sake. But he simply gave her a reassuring smile, and strode off to another computer terminal.

Now what? This was very annoying, Jessica thought. She'd dragged herself here to please him, and now he was taking off and deserting her.

She looked at the screen. There were the words *enter topics* followed by a blinking line. But her mind was a blank. She couldn't imagine finding out about anything she cared about on this Web thing.

Her irritation with Andy was growing. If she told him she wanted to leave now, he'd say she hadn't given this a chance, that she was giving up too quickly. So she'd give it a chance, maybe for about five minutes, and then she'd forget all about this nicey-nicey compromise stuff and insist that he take her home.

She put her hands on the keyboard and typed the first words that came into her mind. *Figure skating*. She hit 'enter'. And she waited for the screen to go blank with frustration.

To her utter amazement, it didn't go blank. Instead, a list appeared. As she scanned the list, her amazement grew. There appeared to be links here to every conceivable aspect of figure skating. Rules and regulations of competition, names of coaches, a directory of rinks, a guide to all medal winners in every major competition since the beginning of the sport.

There were links to pages on specific skaters, too. It seemed that all the famous ones each had a page of their own. She saw the name of her current favourite, Gina Salvatore, an Italian girl she'd watched in the last European competition that was televised. She hadn't won a medal, she'd only come in fifth because she'd missed some jumps, but Jessica had liked her style, which was a little more flamboyant than the usual lady-like skaters.

She moved the cursor to the highlighted name, clicked, and entered. It was incredible. She now had a complete biography of the Italian skater, details of her training and her life and the programmes she'd performed in competition.

At that moment, a box appeared on the screen containing the words *would you like to continue?* She realised her free thirty minutes must be up. She clicked on 'yes'. She was given a password, and she was asked to enter a user name.

She turned. 'Andy?'

He looked away from his screen. 'Yeah?'

'What should I put down for a user name?'

First he looked surprised that she had got that far, and then he looked pleased. 'Anything you want that you can remember,' he told her. 'It's got to be unique, though, so you won't be able to use 'Jessica', except with a number. Mine is Andy513.'

'How did you come up with 513?' she asked him.

'Because my birthday is May 13, and I wouldn't forget that,' he told her. 'Oh, and

I've heard girls say it's a good idea to use a name that doesn't let anyone know if you're a boy or a girl, in case you run into creeps on a chat line.'

She wasn't sure what he meant by that, but for once she took his advice without questioning it. She tried 'Jess', and added the numbers 712, which she figured she'd remember since it signified her birthday, July 12. The name was accepted, and the screen went back to Gina Salvatore.

When she finished looking at all the information about the skater, she considered what she should do next. She decided to check out these chat lines she'd heard about, and clicked on an icon to find out which 'rooms' were currently in session. The menu which appeared listed the rooms under the subjects being discussed.

She noted something called Kids of Divorce, and another group which was listed as Cheerleaders. Neither interested her. There was a gay and lesbian chat line, and another for people who wanted to talk about college entrance exams.

The one that sounded most interesting to her was called Girls Talk About Boys. She clicked into that to see what it was all about.

AliceP: *My boyfriend, Joe, tries to make me jealous by flirting with other girls. I know he really loves me. Why is he doing this?*

Janet49: *Boys are scum.*

Happy: *No, they're not scum, they are just immature. They don't know how to treat a girl.*

SlyFox: *Immature and stupid. Joe thinks AliceP will be impressed because other girls like him. Tell him it isn't working.*

The conversation went on like this, with other girls offering advice to AliceP and others presenting their own hassles with boys. Jessica was enjoying this. It was fun, reading all these gripes about girls who had more problems with their boyfriends than she had.

Impulsively, she decided to join in.

Jess712: *My boyfriend takes me for granted. He expects me to like what he likes.*

She paused before clicking on 'send'. What she had written didn't sound like much of a complaint. She thought for a moment, and then added something with a little more bite.

He orders me around, he makes me do what he wants to do.

She clicked on 'send' and watched in

amazement as her words automatically appeared.

SlyFox: *Don't let him get away with that! Take charge of the relationship!*

AliceP: *Shake him up! Dye your hair, get a tattoo, pierce your nose.*

Janet49: *Pierce your tongue!*

SlyFox: *No, don't pierce anything unless you want to. Don't change yourself. Make him change.*

Jessica grinned. She liked this SlyFox person. And she wouldn't mind hearing her ideas on how she could make some changes in Andy.

But SlyFox and the others were now distracted by a comment from a newcomer who was trying to get a certain boy in her class to notice her. She sounded pretty desperate, and Jessica didn't think it would be nice to interrupt now.

Besides, it was interesting just reading about other people's lives. She'd had no idea that people would reveal so much about themselves to strangers. Of course, the fact that they didn't have to meet face to face was probably a reason people were so open. After all, would she have said in person to anyone what she'd just written on the screen? Especially when it was more or less an outrageous exaggeration?

Andy glanced over towards the computer station where Jessica was sitting, and a warm feeling came over him. Apparently she had found something which appealed to her, because her eyes were fixed on the screen and she was smiling. This pleased him enormously, and he experienced a wave of optimism. Something like this, something they could share, might really work towards improving their relationship.

He turned back to his own screen, and decided to check into his music newsgroups. He subscribed to three of them, each one centred on a particular group he liked.

His absolute favourite was a group devoted to a new, and not very well known, band called Urban, which was just beginning to make some waves. The group's music was political and controversial, and the fans weren't the usual rabid groupies. They weren't great in number yet, but they were the vocal type – intelligent people who enjoyed analyzing and arguing and giving opinions on the music. Once in a while, actual members of the band itself checked into the newsgroup and offered their own comments.

The postings today were interesting, mostly devoted to a cut on the new album.

LPN4: *'Forest for Trees' is right on target. I like how it attacks our feeble attempts at recycling. We're not even making a dent in our environmental problems.*

SAM498: *I don't think that's what the song says. Yes, it says we're not doing enough, but it's not an attack on us. Urban rules!*

TWISTER: *What we're doing is better than nothing. I think Urban should support all efforts to save the environment, even the smallest ones.*

These were typical of the kind of messages you read on the Urban newsgroup. It was the fourth posting that totally surprised him.

KILLER: *Who cares? The environment sucks. Urban sucks. You all suck. You're jerks for listening to this crud group. Grow up.*

He was taken aback. He knew that all newsgroups got *some* cross-postings. People who were on a mission of some sort or another would use every available outlet to spread their views. Sometimes it was religious, sometimes it was political, sometimes it was somebody trying to sell something.

But this couldn't be considered your average cross-posting. This was spamming – a hostile posting that was irrelevant and nasty. He couldn't understand why people did things like this. How could they possibly benefit?

He hoped the other subscribers to the group would do what he planned to do – pay no attention. If you responded to a spammer, he'd just be encouraged to continue. If you ignored him – or her – he might just go away.

But the spam on his favourite newsgroup had put him in a bad mood, and he decided to check on how Jessica was doing. 'Hey, Jess,' he called over to her.

'What?' she called back, her eyes not leaving the screen in front of her.

'What's your screen name?'

'Jess712,' she said.

He put in a request to locate Jess712, and received the information that she was in a chat line, Girls Talk About Boys. *That* sounded intriguing. He entered a message: *Hi, it's me, can I join you?*

He didn't turn to check on Jessica's reaction – he wanted to see if she figured out where this was coming from. He was pleased when a message from her appeared: *Come in!*

He went into the chat line, and started following the discussion.

Janet49: *Boys are so obsessed with themselves. They never think about us.*

Happy: *Everyone knows that girls mature faster than boys. It's a biological fact. So we shouldn't go out with boys our own age.*

AliceP: *All boys of sixteen are worthless.*

SlyFox: *Yeah, let's make a pledge. No more guys under the age of eighteen!*

Andy gaped at the screen. What was going on here?

He felt a presence behind him, and then he heard a voice. 'What's that all about?'

He was annoyed to find Paul Reedy looking over his shoulder and reading his screen. 'It's nothing,' he said, but Paul had already absorbed the strange attack.

'Geez, what a bunch of cows!' he exclaimed.

Andy quickly exited from the chat line, and logged off. 'You shouldn't poke your nose into other people's computers, Paul,' he said, but Paul had already disappeared. He got up and went over to Jessica's station.

'What was that all about?' he asked.

46

Jessica grinned and shrugged. 'I don't know, I guess they get carried away. They have a lot of unusual ideas. You can't blame them, really. I mean, some guys... ' She looked at the screen. 'Like this one, right now!'

Andy looked at the screen and read the line that had just appeared.

BigPaul: *Hey, girls! What's your problem? You haven't met the right kind of sixteen-year-old boy. If you had a real guy in your life, you wouldn't be so angry. Want to meet a really fabulous guy who happens to be sixteen?*

'Oh, no,' Andy groaned. He knew there had to be a million Pauls on the Internet, but he had a suspicion he knew who this one was. He went across the room to where Paul Reedy was at a station.

Sure enough, one look over Paul's shoulder told him Paul was in the Girls Talk About Boys chat line. He was laughing over the responses to his comment.

Janet49: *You evil chauvinist pig!*

SlyFox: *Get out of our room!*

'Paul!' Andy exclaimed. 'What are you doing?'

Paul turned around. 'Hey, you said it's uncool to look at other people's screens.'

Andy rolled his eyes. 'Paul, I think we ought to talk about how you're getting into this stuff. Maybe I could give you some pointers.'

Paul grinned. 'Thanks, man, but I've got it figured out, no sweat.'

'Andy?'

Jessica was standing there. 'I have to get home,' she said. 'It's almost six.'

'OK,' Andy said. He cast another despairing look at Paul, but the class clown had already got out of that chat line and was bothering another group.

As they left together, Andy asked, 'So, how did you like it here?'

'It was interesting,' she replied. 'You were right, it's more interesting than I thought it would be. I found Web sites on figure skaters.'

'Good!' he said. 'That group you were talking to—'

'Yeah,' she broke in. 'That was great!'

He raised his eyebrows. 'You think so?'

'Sure,' she said. 'Maybe they come on a little strong, but it's cool to find girls who talk about guys openly. And it's fun to be able to complain about guys like that.'

He eyed her uneasily. 'Do you feel like you have a lot to complain about?'

'Oh, Andy,' she said, linking her arm through his and laughing.

But she hadn't answered his question.

Chapter Three

At lunchtime the next day, Blair was not in her usual place. She was hiding at a table at the back of the cafeteria. It turned out to be a wasted effort. Her friends were soon able to track her down.

'Blair, what are you doing way back here?' Jessica asked her.

Blair didn't look up from the portable computer she'd set up on the cafeteria table. 'Just a second,' she mumbled, and continued to type.

Jessica and Caryn weren't put off by her lack of welcome. They sat down opposite her, and began unwrapping their sandwiches.

'I can't believe this, you're working at lunchtime,' Caryn commented.

'It's not work,' Blair said, her eyes still on the screen. 'I'm designing a questionnaire. I started it at home last night, and I want to finish it today.'

'A questionnaire about what?' Jessica asked.

'Wait a minute,' Blair said. 'I'm saving

this.' She moved the cursor, hit a key, and then leant back in her chair with a satisfied smile.

Jessica repeated her question. 'What's this questionnaire about?'

'Love,' Blair said. She enjoyed the way Jessica and Caryn gaped at her. And as they both remained speechless, she went on to describe it further.

'This is going to revolutionise my social life,' she told them. 'Not to mention the social life of hundreds, maybe thousands of other girls.'

She could see her two friends exchanging looks of disbelief, but she didn't care. She knew she had just created something brilliant.

'Blair,' Jessica said patiently, 'I know you think computers are the answer to everything. But I honestly doubt that they can make people fall in love.'

'I never said computers are the answer to everything,' Blair stated. 'I said that computers simplify the process, making it easier to get an answer. To get from point A to point B, understand?'

Jessica and Caryn shook their heads.

Blair sighed, and explained. 'Point A is a person alone. Point B is a person in a relationship with another person, a relationship that's mutually satisfying, without any fear that the relationship is a waste of time. You want to know how it works?'

'Sure,' her friends said in unison, though they both still looked extremely sceptical.

'It's actually very simple. Before two people go out on a date, they fill out the questionnaire, responding to each statement with a number from one to five. One means "not at all", two is "don't care either way", three is "somewhat", four is "yes", five is "very much".'

She looked back at the computer screen. 'Here's an example. One statement says, "I like to dance." If the girl marks five and the boy marks one, they're obviously not meant for each other.'

'Oh, come on,' Jessica objected. 'You think dancing is that important to everyone?'

'Of course not,' Blair replied. 'But if it wasn't important, both would have marked three. A two and a four might get along if they're willing to compromise. But a five and a one? No way.'

Caryn shook her head. 'I still don't think you can base a whole relationship on whether or not you like to dance.'

'I realise that,' Blair replied. 'There are two hundred and fifty statements on this questionnaire.' She grinned as their mouths dropped open.

'It's not just about dancing,' she explained. 'I cover everything from favourite foods to sleeping habits.'

'You're kidding!' Caryn practically shrieked. 'You're asking people about *sex*?'

Blair gave her a pained look. 'No, silly, I said sleeping habits. For example, there's a statement that declares "Sleeping late on weekends is important to me." Now, if someone likes to sleep late, that person won't be happy with someone who calls at nine o'clock on a Saturday morning. Or with someone who likes to go fishing.'

'Fishing?' Jessica asked. 'You ask if people are interested in fishing?'

Blair nodded. 'I cover everything.'

'What are you going to do with this questionnaire?' Jessica asked. 'Pass it around at school?'

'It's not just for here,' Blair declared. 'I'm going to cover the entire country. Anyone between the ages of fifteen and seventeen can take part.'

Caryn looked horrified. 'You're going to

match up strangers? Isn't that dangerous?'

Blair groaned. 'Caryn, this isn't a match-making service, and I'm not trying to bring people together. This is for people who are already going out together, or thinking about it. This questionnaire prevents them from making a terrible mistake and having a lot of misery later on.'

Now, both Jessica and Caryn wore blank, uncomprehending expressions. Blair was beginning to think her friends weren't very bright.

Blair tried to explain. 'Say there's a couple who have gone out once or twice, or maybe they're just considering a date. Well, they can find out if they're ultimately suited. Right from the start, they'll know whether or not their relationship has a chance of making it. They won't waste time going out on dates that will lead nowhere.'

Jessica interrupted her. 'You think going out on a date is a waste of time?'

'Sure,' Blair said. 'If it leads to one person being dumped and feeling awful. The real problem is that people usually begin a relationship based on a purely physical attraction.'

'Yeah, so what?' Caryn asked.

'Well, that might carry them through for

a few weeks, but that kind of attraction is going to wear off. Once they've filled out this questionnaire, they'll know if they're really compatible in the long run. And no one will get hurt. It's like having a guarantee!'

Jessica eyed her quizzically. 'Satisfaction guaranteed or your money back, huh?'

'No money is going to change hands,' Blair declared solemnly. 'This is a service project. It's my contribution to a better world.'

'What about chemistry?' Jessica asked.

It was Blair's turn to go blank. 'Chemistry?'

'Yeah, chemistry. You know, that spark, the element of magic, that mysterious thing that just seems to happen when two people look at each other and they know they're meant for each other.'

Blair frowned. 'That's not chemistry. Chemistry is a science. What you're talking about is animal magnetism. It is not reliable to act on instinct.'

'Blair, I'm sorry, but this all sounds very weird to me,' Caryn declared.

Jessica nodded in agreement. 'You can't change human nature.'

'Wanna bet?' Blair responded.

She realised that lunchtime was almost over when she saw Andy coming their way.

'What are you guys doing way back here?' he asked when he arrived at their table.

'Ask Blair,' Caryn commented.

'No, maybe he'd better not,' Jessica said. 'Unless he's got all day to listen.'

Blair ignored that. 'I've worked up a questionnaire to establish the potential success of a relationship between a boy and a girl,' she told Andy. She went on to explain the project to him.

Andy didn't belittle her, but he didn't look impressed either. In fact, his reaction was a little peculiar. '*I* don't need anything like that,' he blurted out, looking strangely unnerved as he glanced at Jessica.

'I haven't said you did,' Blair replied. 'But some people do. And actually, I don't think it would hurt any couple to fill out the questionnaire and find out if they're really meant to be together.' She looked meaningfully at Andy and then at Jessica as she spoke. She thought they might make an interesting test case.

'No thanks,' Jessica replied. She turned to Andy. 'Are you going to the Double Click Café this afternoon?'

'I don't know, I've got a debate club meeting after school,' he said.

'Can we go after that?' she persisted. 'I'll wait for you in the media centre.'

'I'll be at the Double Click this afternoon,' Blair said. 'I want to design a homepage so people can access the questionnaire.'

'Remind me to show you this cool group of girls I found on an Internet chat line,' Jessica told her.

Blair rose and picked up her computer. 'OK. I have to run, I need to go to the media centre before class and copy the questionnaire on to a diskette.'

That afternoon, at the Double Click Café, Blair created her homepage and uploaded the questionnaire on to it. She explained its purpose, and gave specific instructions as to how it should be filled out.

'Entries may be anonymous, if desired,' she typed, 'but each pair of questionnaires should have the same code number so that they can be analyzed together. Each couple who submits a completed questionnaire will receive a response within twenty-four hours, indicating the degree of probability that the relationship can be successful.'

She thought the idea of having her own

homepage was a great way to make the questionnaire easily available to anyone with a modem. People could fill in the questionnaire on the screen and e-mail it directly back to her. But now she had to come up with a way to publicise the address of the homepage so people would know it existed.

She decided the best means would be to advertise on the newsgroups that were popular with kids their age. She could give a brief description, something that would arouse their curiosity, and the address where they could learn more about it in detail and actually find the questionnaire.

She had some qualms about spreading the information through newsgroups. It would mean doing a lot of cross-posting, which was generally frowned upon. But she decided that this was a situation where the ends justified the means.

She was doing this for a good cause. Hundreds, thousands of girls – and boys too – would ultimately thank her for thinking of this.

She was already thanking herself. Never again would she suffer as she had in the past, falling for some totally unsuitable guy, giving her heart to someone who just wasn't right for her. Before she did so much as step out of her front door to greet someone, she'd make him fill out the questionnaire first. She was going to save herself and many other people, a lot of heartache.

She decided to subscribe to thirty newsgroups she thought would be popular with kids her age, mostly ones dealing with music groups and Television shows. She kept the postings brief and to the point.

'Is he Mr Right or Mr Wrong? Is she the girl of your dreams or your nightmares? Find out for sure with the Love Test.'

She figured that was enough to catch someone's eye and, she hoped, make them curious, so she simply added the address of her homepage.

She'd been sitting hunched over the computer for almost an hour now, and she needed to stretch. As she got up and moved around, she saw something she hadn't noticed before – a bulletin board. She went over to examine it.

There were notices to other kids who hung out here, and lots of announcements about interesting new Web sites and stuff. She hurried back to her computer, printed out a copy of her Love Test announcement, and brought it back with her to the bulletin board.

It was while she was searching for a drawing pin that she had the sensation of someone just behind her. Then she heard a male voice.

'A love test?'

She found a pin, and started looking for a good space on the board as she responded. 'I know,' she mumbled, 'it's a silly name but I couldn't think of anything else.'

'What is it?'

She secured the paper to the board, turned and faced the speaker. 'It's… it's, well, I guess it's not really a test. It's a questionnaire. Sort of. I mean, it definitely is a questionnaire. For people who are, you know, going together. Or want to go out, or something. To, you know, see if it's, uh, you know, OK.'

She hadn't had any difficulty before, explaining this to Jessica and Caryn and Andy. She didn't know why she was stumbling over her words now.

But maybe she did know why. This guy, this total stranger, had the bluest eyes she'd ever seen. They crinkled when he smiled, like he was smiling now. She had an instinctive feeling that he smiled a lot. A lock of sandy-coloured hair was hanging down his forehead, almost covering one of those eyes, and she impulsively wanted to push it back. She didn't, of course, but she could feel the desire.

Then she became aware of a frighteningly familiar, hollow sensation in the pit of her stomach. She took a deep breath, steeled herself, and remembered her vow. Never again.

He was still looking at the notice, and saying, 'I don't understand this, why—'

She interrupted. 'If you want to know more, the homepage address is on the announcement.' With that, she turned and resolutely walked away.

'Did you like that CD I was playing in the car?' Andy asked Jessica as they walked through the parking lot towards the Double Click Café.

'Yeah, it was nice,' Jessica said. 'I guess I wasn't really listening, though.'

'Oh. Well, anyway, that's the band I was telling you about, Urban. There's a good newsgroup about them if you want to check it out.'

'Sure, maybe later,' Jessica said, but he didn't think she was really serious. He had a feeling she was more interested in getting back to that guy-bashing group. The moment they got inside the café, she took off for a computer station, sat down, and logged on. Apparently, she didn't even need his help any more.

He watched her for a moment, thinking that he should be satisfied and proud that she'd picked up on this so quickly, with so much enthusiasm, and wondering why he didn't feel better about it.

He sat down and tried to concentrate on his own stuff. He logged on and went into his Urban newsgroup, where most of the messages were centring on the band's recent announcement that they were donating half the proceeds of a tour to a particular political candidate.

Music is music, it shouldn't take sides and try to be political.

Music is supposed to be political. Think about the music of the late 1960s, like Jefferson Airplane, Bob Dylan and all that.

This isn't the 60s, this is the 90s. Times have changed.

You ever heard of freedom of speech? It's

guaranteed to all Americans, even rock bands. Urban has the right to support a candidate publicly.

Urban is using its popularity to influence people. They're abusing their position.

Andy was glad to see that the subscribers to the group were ignoring yesterday's spam. But unfortunately, this didn't stop the spammer.

Hey, weasels! Do you really take this rot seriously? You should change the name of your group from alt.music.Urban to alt.brain.damage! Or maybe you're all junkies and you groove on this peace and love garbage.

Once again, the message came from someone who called himself Killer.

What was this guy's problem, Andy wondered. Whoever he was, he'd probably never even listened to Urban, he just wanted to start a cyber-fight, get a reaction. This posting sounded nastier than the first one – it was getting personal, and more like a real flame. Subscribers to a newsgroup might be able to ignore the occasional stupid spam, but flaming could get them very angry.

He glanced back at Jessica. He wanted to show this to her, get her reaction, but she was deeply engrossed in her own group. Impulsively, he sent her an instant message.

Hi, what are you doing?

I'm in my chat line.

So now it was *her* chat line. Well, if this was what she cared about, maybe he should try harder to understand it. He sent another message.

Can I come in and meet your friends?

OK.

It wasn't exactly an invitation, but at least he had permission. He went into the chat room, and introduced himself to the occupants.

Hi. I'm Andy. I'm a friend of Jessica's.

There was an immediate response.

SlyFox: *Are you the boyfriend?*

He was pleased to know that she had described him to the group that way.

Yes.

But the responses that followed this were totally unexpected.

Janet49: *Stop pushing her around!*

Happy: *She can live without you.*

AliceP: *Better watch out. Girls don't have to take this from boys.*

He stared at the screen in bewilderment. Had he missed something? Had someone said something nasty just before he came into the room? He recalled that Paul Reedy had made an obnoxious statement in this group yesterday. Had he reappeared just before Andy came on the scene?

But the next remark told him for sure that the angry comments weren't aimed at anyone but him.

SlyFox: *You'd better shape up, Andy. Or you'll lose that girl.*

This did nothing to help lift his confusion. He left his station and went over to where Jessica was sitting. She had her eyes glued to the screen. Obviously, she was aware of what they'd been saying to him. He was relieved to note she wasn't smiling.

'Jess?'

She turned to him.

'What's going on?' he asked her.

'I don't know,' she replied.

'I don't push you around,' he said. 'Do I?'

She shook her head slightly.

'Then why are they yelling at me like this? What did you tell them about me?'

A small, abashed smile appeared on her face. 'Well, we were talking about our boyfriends, and I guess I exaggerated a little.'

He said nothing, waiting for more explanation.

She shrugged. 'Well, you *do* have some strong opinions, Andy.'

'So do you,' he replied.

'Yeah. Well… ' She looked again at the screen.

'Would you tell them to stop?' he asked.

Her fingers began hitting the keys. He went back to his own screen to see if she was telling them the truth about what a nice guy he was.

Jess712: *Gotta go.*

He kept watching the screen to see if that was all she was going to write.

AliceP: *This is such a great group! You all make me feel empowered!*

Happy: *I actually feel sorry for any boys who come in this room.*

Janet49: *Maybe what they need is a Boys Talk About Girls chat line.*

AliceP: *That's what locker rooms are for!*

SlyFox: *Here's a place we can send the boys who want to talk about girls.*

Some letters appeared, and Andy recognised them as the beginning of an address for a newsgroup. The words that followed were *relationships.advice.*

As the conversation continued, the

address began to move up the screen. Andy grabbed a pencil and jotted it down on his notebook cover before it disappeared.

Chapter Four

Jessica felt a little strange walking into the Double Click Café that evening. She had a sensation she hadn't had since she was a little girl, when she used to sneak down to the kitchen after her parents were in bed to take a forbidden cookie. She felt as if she was doing something naughty, as if she was sneaking around behind Andy's back.

Which was ridiculous, of course. There was absolutely no reason why she couldn't come here by herself. It wasn't as though she was doing something illegal, or meeting another guy. She didn't need to feel guilty, just because Andy had turned her on to the place.

But she couldn't help having this nagging sensation that she shouldn't be here, not without him, not without him knowing she was here. Maybe she felt bad because her chat line pals attacked him earlier that day. But she hadn't told them to do that.

She might have given them the ammunition, though. After all, she had been telling them stuff about Andy, things he did and didn't do that annoyed her.

The Double Click Café wasn't nearly as crowded in the evening as it was in the afternoon. Hilary waved at her from behind the bar and she waved back. Then she sat down at a station and logged on.

She went into her chat line and looked at the square on the top of the screen that indicated who was in the room at that time. She didn't recognise any of the user names she'd seen in her other sessions in the room. She figured that people probably went online around the same time every day, as she'd been doing.

She began reading the discussion that was crossing the screeen.

SusiQ: *Are all men morons or just my boyfriend?*

LadyBlue: *They're not morons, they're idiots.*

RSK23: *Here's a joke I heard. What do you call a man with half a brain? Gifted.*

Jessica didn't think that was particularly funny. If there was one thing she would never complain about, it was Andy's intelligence.

The people online at the moment were boring. She left her station and went over to the bar. Just as Hilary took her order for a soda, Greg appeared.

Hilary smiled radiantly at him, and Greg kissed her on the cheek.

'I'll take over now,' he said. 'You're tired.'

'I look that bad, huh?' she asked.

'No, you look beautiful,' he replied. 'Tired, yes, but always beautiful.'

Jessica tried to imagine Andy talking like that to her, telling her she was beautiful. That was definitely something about Andy that bugged her. He never gave her any compliments, he never noticed how she looked.

She finished the soda and went back to her station. There, she realised she hadn't exited and she was still logged on to the chat line. Now she'd have to pay for the fifteen minutes she spent drinking the soda.

She was about to get out of the chat line when a name appeared that she recognised.

SlyFox: *Hey, Jess712, are you there?*

She must have seen Jessica's user name in the box at the top of the screen. Quickly, she responded.

Jess712: *Yes, I'm here.*

SlyFox: *Your boyfriend is Andy513, right?*

Jess712: *Right. Why?*

SlyFox: *I just saw his name, he's posted a message in the relationship advice news group. Maybe you should check it out, see what he's talking about.*

She provided the address of the news-group.

Jess712: *Thanks, I will.*

She exited from the chat line, but she didn't go into anything else right away. She went offline, and thought.

That was odd. What would Andy be doing in an advice newsgroup? She was uncomfortably aware of a cold shiver down her back. Were things between them worse than she thought they were? Her thoughts went back to the warnings she'd received from Blair about how relationships required sharing and compromise.

OK, she'd been trying to share his interests. Wasn't she here right now, at his favourite place, the Double Click Café? But she had to be honest with herself. She wasn't really sharing anything with him. And maybe he *was* getting sick of the 'discussions', like Caryn had suggested.

It would be easy enough to find out what he'd posted, what kind of advice he wanted. All she had to do was subscribe to the newsgroup and read the messages. He wouldn't know she was spying on him.

Still, she hesitated. Maybe she was better off *not* knowing what he was asking. It might not have anything to do with her, anyway. The news group probably dealt with all kinds of relationships, not just romantic ones. Jessica knew that Andy often argued with his father. And he was very competitive with his brother, who was two years older. He might very well be looking for advice on how to deal with them. He deserved his privacy.

But even as she was talking herself out of it, her hand touched the mouse and began moving the cursor towards a certain icon – the one which could put her in the general area of newsgroups. She clicked.

Now all she needed to do was type in the address of the group and hit 'enter'. But if she did that, what would she find there?

She imagined the message. *I've been going out with the same girl for four months, and she's really getting on my nerves. We argue all the time, and I'm sick and tired of it. I want to break up with her, but I don't want to hurt her feelings. What can I do?*

Then she tried to imagine life without Andy. For all their problems, she couldn't imagine feeling as comfortable with any other boy in the world. She wondered what was worse – her imagination or the reality?

She decided that not knowing anything at all was the scariest.

She pressed her lips together tightly. She typed out the address. And she hit 'enter'.

A message appeared: *You have been subscribed to this newsgroup.*

Then she moved the cursor to the icon labelled My Newsgroups, and clicked. Since she hadn't subscribed to any other newsgroups, the only name that appeared on the screen was the relationship advice newsgroup. She moved the cursor to that, and clicked again.

What appeared then was a long list of sub-topics on the subject of relationships. What had Andy called them? Threads – right, that's what they were.

She scanned the threads, brief statements that described what the messages in that category were about:

My mother nags me.
My sister is bossy.
I hate my brother.
I had a fight with my best friend.
I'm in love with my best friend's boyfriend.
Next to each thread was a number which

indicated the number of postings on that particular sub-topic. There were no names to indicate who wrote them.

Then how had SlyFox known that Andy had posted a message, she wondered. She realised that SlyFox must have actually read what Andy had written. Now she was even more alarmed. If SlyFox had known what Andy's message said when she told Jessica to check it out, that meant the message definitely had something to do with her.

Her eyes moved down the screen, reading the threads. She paused at one: *A problem with my girlfriend*. There were three messages attached to it. She moved the arrow to that one and clicked.

And there it was: *Message 1 of 3*.

I've been with my girlfriend for four months. I really love her. I think she loves me too, but I don't think she's happy with me. I'm afraid I'm going to lose her. What can I do? Andy513

Jessica felt like she could melt with relief. How terribly sweet he sounded – not angry, not even annoyed, just sweet and a little sad. It made her want to cry.

She was curious to see what kind of advice he'd been offered by other subscribers to the newsgroup. She clicked on the Next Message square.

Don't crawl around trying to make some chick happy. Be a man, dump her. Bag the hag. Killer.

Creepy, she thought. She clicked again to bring up the next one.

Give her a present. Like jewellery. Or a box of chocolates. WRB29.

She hoped he wouldn't be taking the advice either of those subscribers offered. She didn't want to be dumped. She knew Andy couldn't afford to spend money on jewellery, and it would make her feel guilty if he did. She was watching her figure, so she didn't want chocolates. She hunched over the screen, figured out how to go back to previous messages, and read the original request for advice.

It was too bad *she* couldn't tell him what to do.

Then she sat upright. Why couldn't she? Why couldn't she post a message of her own on this thread and tell him exactly what he could do to make his girlfriend happy? She certainly knew better than anyone else what she wanted.

But then he'd know she'd been spying on him. At the end of every posting, the user name was provided, and Andy knew who Jess712 was. Maybe he'd think it was cute and funny that she was telling him what to do. Or maybe not. She wasn't sure that she wanted to take that risk.

She leant back in her chair to think. She noticed Greg, bent over a boy two stations away, showing him how to do something. Now that was a guy who knew how to treat a girlfriend, Jessica thought.

When the boy nodded, looking satisfied, Greg stood upright, and caught Jessica's eye. He must have thought her expression meant she needed something, because he asked, 'What can I do for you?'

'Actually,' Jessica said, 'I do have a question. Can a person change his user name?'

'Let me see what server you're using,' Greg said. Quickly, Jessica got out of the newsgroup before Greg reached her and bent down to examine her screen.

'Well, you can't literally change it,' he said. 'But you can add other user names and operate under those. Just go back to the original set-up...' He showed Jessica how she could add other names to her original one, and send messages under any name.

She thanked him, he left her, and she considered what to do next. First off, she needed a name, something that would mean nothing to Andy. She didn't want some cute nickname, because she didn't think he would take any advice seriously if it came from someone with a goofy name.

She wasn't sure if it would be better to pose as a boy or a girl, so she decided again to use a name that could go both ways. Chris would be good, she thought, but there must be hundreds of Chrises on line. She'd need a number, something she could remember.

It came to her, and she grinned. She typed in her new name: Chris1492. There was no way she could forget that. Back in the second grade, a teacher had made her class memorize the words: In fourteen hundred and ninety-two, Columbus sailed the ocean blue. She'd never forgotten it.

Using the new name, she subscribed again to the advice newsgroup. She went into the thread Andy had started, and clicked on Post Message.

Now what? What *did* she want from Andy, really? Simply telling him to pay more attention to his girlfriend was too vague. She needed to be more specific, and find out if he was really willing to take advice.

She decided to start off with something very simple.

Speak romantically to her. Give her some compliments. Tell her she's beautiful. Chris1492.

She read it over and almost laughed out loud. She decided she didn't feel the least bit guilty because what she was doing wasn't really naughty. Besides, it would be very interesting to see if he actually took the advice.

The next day, for Blair, was interminable. She'd never known a school day to pass so slowly. In each class period, she must have looked at her watch a hundred times, decided it had stopped and then compared the time on the watch to the clock on the wall. They were always the same.

When the final bell rang, she tore out of her class and hurried out of the building. She stood on the steps for a moment, trying to decide whether to walk or take the bus to the Double Click Café. She was debating which was the better option, when Andy approached her.

'Need a ride?' he asked.

'I want to go to the Double Click Café,' she told him.

'Me too,' he said, and she followed him out into the parking lot to his car.

'Where's Jess?' she asked as she got in.

'Running errands for her mother,' he said.

'What kind of errands?'

'How should I know? She doesn't tell me everything she does.' He sounded almost irritable, so Blair didn't press the question. She was still hoping to get the two of them to take her Love Test, but she felt reasonably sure she knew what the result would be. They were the weirdest couple she'd ever seen in her life.

When they walked into the Double Click Café, Andy was greeted with a whoop. 'Yo, Shaw, my main man! What's the story, what's happening, hit me with some news!'

The greeting came from Paul Reedy, who was striding towards them. Andy looked pained, and Blair could understand why. Paul could be a major jerk, always fooling around in class, trying to be funny and getting on people's nerves. She had no desire to listen to him now.

'Thanks for the ride,' she murmured to

Andy, and took off for a station.

She tried to stay calm as she logged on. In her instructions, she'd told her potential clients to send the completed questionnaires to her e-mail address, so the first thing she did was to check her e-mail.

After clicking on to her mailbox, she watched the signals at the bottom of the screen. Calling... Sign On... Checking Inbox... And then it read Retrieving 6.

Don't get too excited, she cautioned herself. This could be ordinary e-mail, from out of town friends. Then the lines indicating who had sent the messages began to appear, one after another. There were six names, all unfamiliar. And for each, the subject stated: Love Test.

Excitedly, she took a quick look at each one. All had followed the procedure correctly, and by the coding she could tell which two were to be analysed together. She downloaded each pair of questionnaires on to a diskette, and then uploaded the data into the analysis program she'd saved on the hard drive. She set the program in motion.

A short time later she was printing out the results. The disparity between each couple's responses had been measured and tabulated. Incredible, she thought. In less than five minutes, she had solved the romantic plights of three couples.

She was dying to begin studying the print-outs. She had designed a measuring tool – all she had to do was look at the ultimate number each relationship had acquired, and see where it fell in the measurement table. A score over fifty meant that the relationship had a good chance of working out. The lower the score, the less likely that there would be compatability between the two people involved.

But she was feeling so good, so pleased with herself, that she didn't object when she was interrupted before she could begin.

'How's the Love Test going?'

She turned towards the voice. It was the guy from yesterday, the one with the eyes.

'Very well, thank you,' she replied. 'I've had six responses. That's three couples.'

'I can do simple division,' he said with a smile. 'By the way, I'm Sean Douglas.' He put out his right hand, and she took it in hers.

'I'm Blair Moorehead,' she offered,

thinking that most guys she knew wouldn't dream of shaking hands when they met a girl. It was considered too polite. Personally, she thought this was cool.

'Pleased to meet you,' he said.

'Same here,' she replied. 'You don't go to Briarcliff High, do you?'

'No, I'm at Lakeside. Junior class.'

'I'm a junior at Briarcliff,' Blair told him. This was followed by the usual awkward moment, where neither could think of anything to say. Blair usually resolved this by asking about the courses at the other school.

'Do you have to take that awful life-saving course in phys. ed. at Lakeside?' she asked.

'Drown-proofing? Yeah, I'm taking it now. It's required in the junior year.'

'Same for us,' Blair said.

'You know why it's called drown-proofing, don't you?' Sean asked.

'No...'

'Because it proves that you're capable of drowning,' he said, smiling.

It wasn't much of a joke, but the way he said it made her smile, too.

'Tell me more about this Love Test,' he said. 'I know, I could have accessed your homepage, but I was just too lazy. Besides, I'd rather get a personal version from the creator's own lips.'

His honesty was charming. Today she found herself able to speak without stuttering. 'It's something I designed to help people from falling in love with the wrong person. If you think you like someone, or if you've just started dating someone, you can each take the test and find out if the relationship is worth pursuing.'

'You mean, *you* decide if this couple should go out together?'

'No, the computer decides. I designed a program to analyse the data. Then I e-mail the results to the couple.'

'And then what?' he asked.

She shrugged. 'I don't know, that's their decision. I assume that if they learn that they're not meant for each other, they'll stop going out.'

His eyes registered disbelief. 'You think they're going to change their feelings based on what you tell them?'

'Based on what the *computer* tells them,' she corrected him. 'This is based on logic, not feelings.'

'I see,' he said thoughtfully.

'Would you like to fill out the questionnaire?' she asked. 'It's free.' She paused, and then added, 'Of course, it can only be analysed in pairs, so someone else would need to take the questionnaire too.'

He grinned. 'No, thanks. I have to run, maybe I'll see you here tomorrow.'

She nodded, realising she wasn't terribly disappointed that he didn't want to fill out her questionnaire. Because maybe that meant he wasn't very interested in any particular girl at the moment.

She went back to study the analysis of the questionnaire from the three couples. She wanted to e-mail the results to her clients today.

Andy killed half an hour checking his usual newsgroups. He'd managed to shake Paul Reedy, telling him he had serious work to do, but that didn't stop the jerk from lurking around, reading over Andy's shoulder.

'Look, Paul, I've really got to concentrate,' he said, trying not to sound too hostile. Paul finally moved on to annoy someone else.

There was more flaming on the Urban newsgroup, from Killer, of course.

Hey, you slime-buckets! Don't you have anything better to do with your lives than listen to half-baked musical crap? Did you know that every time you listen to an Urban song you lose five thousand brain cells? I don't think you guys can afford to lose any more!

Today, for the first time, there was a response to the flame.

It wasn't written in the same illogical manner. The people who were into Urban's music were too cool for that. They weren't online amateurs, either. People who were serious online participants knew about netiquette, and they knew what could happen if you responded online to flamers. It would only encourage them.

But apparently, one person had simply had enough and couldn't ignore this idiot any longer. His comment was terse and to the point.

Killer, get out of our newsgroup.

Andy doubted that this message would do any good. But he could sympathise with the guy who wrote it. He'd just about had enough himself.

He'd been putting off doing what he really wanted to do online this afternoon. Now he'd exhausted all other resources for killing time, and he had to check into the Relationship Advice newsgroup.

First, he made sure no one like Paul Reedy was watching over his shoulder. No, Paul was looking over someone else's shoulder at the moment. The victim turned and caught him, and he made no effort to be as nice as Andy when he responded to the intrusion on his privacy.

'Hey, get out of my face!' he barked at Paul.

Paul stepped backwards, his hands up in a position of mock self-defence. 'Whoa, excuse me for living! Look, man, if you want to send letters threatening to burn down The White House and kidnap the President of the United States, that's none of my business!'

He started laughing at his own joke. Nobody else did. Greg approached Paul and spoke in a low voice that Andy couldn't hear, but he had a pretty good idea what Greg was telling him. From his serious, almost stern expression, Greg was clearly issuing some sort of warning to Paul about his obnoxious behaviour.

Andy returned to his screen, accessed the newsgroup, and brought up the responses to his request for advice. The first one startled him, and not just because of the advice to *dump her* and *bag the hag*. It was the name of the adviser that surprised him: Killer. The same name used by the flamer in his Urban newsgroup.

He looked at it uneasily. What did this mean? Was this Killer person following him? Was something personal going on here, or just a weird coincidence?

It had to be coincidence, he decided. If Killer was angry with Andy about something, he'd be sending nasty e-mails, not flaming newsgroups. This was just a fluke. If he checked into other newsgroups, ones he didn't normally subscribe to, he'd probably find Killer there, too. Obviously, the guy didn't have much of a life.

He went on to the next bit of advice on the thread. *Buy her a present*... Well, that was more realistic. But he couldn't afford any jewellery right now, and he didn't think Jessica would go wild over chocolates, especially since she'd been talking about being on a diet.

He hoped he'd find something better in the last posting in the thread.

Speak romantically to her... Compliment her... Tell her she's beautiful.

He looked at the words thoughtfully.

That was simple enough. Privately, he thought Jessica was too down-to-earth and matter-of-fact to be swept away by compliments – but you never knew.

OK, Chris1492, he said silently to the sender. I'll give it a try.

Chapter Five

Jessica saw Andy waiting by her locker when she arrived at school the next morning. She was a little surprised – it wasn't a typical habit of his, since he was usually running late for school and his own locker was on the other side of the school building. She wondered what he had to tell her that was so important it couldn't wait until lunchtime.

'Hi,' she greeted him, cheerfully. 'What's up?'

'Nothing's up,' he replied quickly. 'I just wanted to see you.'

'Really? Why?'

'Well, I guess because I haven't seen you for a while. Not since, since…'

Jessica finished the sentence for him. 'Not since yesterday at lunch.'

He shrugged and smiled a little oddly. 'Well, you know, it seems longer. Like… like forever.'

Jessica blinked, and wondered if she'd heard him correctly. 'Huh?'

'I missed you,' he said. 'And I can't stop

thinking about you.'

She gaped. 'Yeah?'

He nodded. 'You look very beautiful today.'

Now she was very confused. She wasn't wearing anything special, there was nothing out of the ordinary about the way she looked at that moment...

Then she gasped. He was doing it! He was taking her advice from the newsgroup!

'What's the matter?' Andy asked in alarm.

She started coughing, to give herself time to think. He continued to stare at her, the expression of concern growing.

'There's something in my throat,' she managed by way of explanation.

He came towards her. 'I know the Heimlich manoeuvre,' he said, his arms open.

She jumped back. 'No! It's OK now.'

'Are you sure?'

'Yes, absolutely.'

'You know, I've been thinking about something,' Andy said. 'Remember, how we talked about going to the basketball game Saturday night?'

She nodded. Not being a basketball fan, she hadn't been looking forward to it.

'Instead of that, maybe we could do something alone. Just the two of us. What do you think?'

She was stunned. Andy was going to give up a basketball game to be alone with her? She tried to sound nonchalant, but it wasn't easy.

'OK,' she said. 'My parents are going out. Why don't you come over and I'll make dinner? I've got a recipe for home-made pizza.'

'Great,' he said. 'I'll bring a video.'

She was about to suggest one, a love story she'd been wanting to see, but she held her tongue. It would be interesting to see what he would choose for an evening alone.

'Fine,' she said.

'Well, I'll, um, see you at lunch,' he said, and he took off. She stood there, watching him walk away. She must have had a pretty idiotic grin on her face, because when Charlie Kingston, her classmate, walked by, she said, 'Are you practising to be a clown?'

She said it in a friendly way. Charlie wasn't a particularly close friend of Jessica's, but they knew each other from classes, and had exchanged bits of gossip now and then. And Jessica had a major urge to confide her little prank to somebody. She couldn't tell Blair or Caryn, she'd just get a lecture about honesty, but Charlie had always struck her as someone who liked to flirt mischievously.

So Jessica told her what she'd done to Andy, and how Andy had responded that morning. Charlie definitely appreciated the story.

'That's wild!' she laughed. 'Too cool! But look, you shouldn't stop now. You've got power! Keep sending him advice on that newsgroup. You could turn him into whatever you want him to be! You could create the perfect boyfriend!'

'Oh, come on,' Jessica remonstrated. 'I couldn't do that, I'm not *that* manipulative.'

'Why not?' Charlie said, still laughing as she moved on down the hall. 'He took your advice the first time, didn't he? See how far he'll go!'

She was just joking, Jessica knew that. But it was an intriguing idea. Andy was starting to act more romantic. What else could she get him to do?

On Sunday morning, Blair was up by nine

o'clock. She climbed out of bed and immediately went to the phone, where she dialled the number of the Double Click Café.

The ringing was answered by a recording. Blair recognised Greg's voice.

'Hello, you have reached the Double Click Café. We are open from ten until midnight, Monday through Friday, and from noon until midnight on Saturday and Sunday.'

She hung up the phone. Damn, she thought. What was she going to do between now and noon? She was dying to get to the café and see if she'd had any response to the reports she'd sent out to her clients.

Of the three couples who'd e-mailed their questionnaires, one had received a high degree of probability that their relationship would be a success. Another couple was almost as good. Only one couple had received a warning – any movement towards romance on their part would put them on the road to disaster.

She'd asked all of them to confirm receiving their reports, and to let her know the results of any interaction between them. The reports had been sent out on

Thursday. She hadn't heard anything back yet. But now a weekend had passed, she should be getting reports of some sort.

She wished she had her own modem at home so she could access her e-mail. She was feeling restless, with nothing to do. She'd done all her weekend homework, and she was up to date on her term projects. It had been a very quiet weekend.

She dialled Jessica's number. A reluctant voice, thick with sleep, responded. 'Hello?'

'Hi, Jess, it's me.'

After a moment's silence, Jessica said, 'Blair, you know I like to sleep late on Sundays.'

'Sorry, I'll call you back later.'

There was the sound of a yawn. 'Never mind, I'm awake now. What's going on?'

'Nothing. What did you do this weekend?'

'Andy came over last night. I made a pizza. We watched videos.'

'You don't sound very enthusiastic,' Blair commented.

'It was OK,' Jessica said. 'But I forgot that he hates green peppers, and I put them all over the pizza. And the videos he brought starred Jean-Claude van Damme and Sylvester Stallone.'

'Yuck,' Blair said.

'Yeah, you get the idea.'

'Sounds like a fun evening.'

'*Not*. What are you doing today?'

'I'm going to the Double Click Café at noon,' Blair told her. 'You want to meet me?'

'Yeah, OK,' Jessica replied.

Blair spent the rest of the morning cleaning her room and organising her wardrobe, sending her mother into a state of ecstasy. At precisely noon, she was in front of the Double Click Café. Just as Hilary unlocked the door, Jessica appeared.

'Is Andy coming here today?' Blair asked her. After her conversation with Jessica that morning, she was even more determined to get the two of them to take her questionnaire and realise what a dismal couple they were.

'Maybe later,' Jessica said. 'He had to go and visit his grandmother this morning.'

Blair noticed that even though the Double Click Café was empty, Jessica chose a station several seats away from her's – obviously, she wanted privacy. Blair wondered what she was up to.

Maybe she had an e-mail relationship going on, a long-distance romance. That was good, Blair thought. It might make her re-think her useless relationship with Andy. She didn't like the idea of Andy being hurt, but he'd be better off in the long run.

She checked her e-mail, and was notified that one message was being retrieved. She watched the screen anxiously, waiting for the retrieval to be identified.

The line that appeared read: *From: Ellen Crenshaw/Subject: Love Test.*

Her heart leapt. She recognised the name – it was one of her questionnaire participants. She checked in her notebook, where she was keeping a record of everything. Ellen Crenshaw was half of couple number one, with the highest probability of success.

She opened the message.

Dear Love Test, Are you for real or what? I didn't want to go out with this guy who's been after me, but he saw your announcement. I told him if we matched up, I'd go out with him. You said we were a match made in heaven and I was stupid enough to believe you. The night turned out to be the date from hell. OK, maybe we both like playing tennis, but that was it. And that's not just my opinion. Believe me, he'd be telling you the same thing.

Blair frowned. Certainly, the couple must have had more in common than tennis or she – the computer, actually – would never have given the relationship such high marks for potential success.

This was bizarre, it didn't make any sense. She wanted to review the questionnaire and the analysis program. There had to be a glitch somewhere.

But first she called up the report she'd sent the couple, just to make sure it hadn't been misinterpreted. But the report to Ellen Crenshaw was very clear.

The potential for an excellent relationship is here. You've got a match made in heaven. Everything checks out, you two are perfectly suited for each other. So don't hesitate. Get together!

Then she called up Ellen Crenshaw's questionnaire, to see if something had gone wrong there. As she waited, a voice behind her said, 'Hi!'

Reluctantly, she turned from the screen. It was Sean, from Lakeside High.

'Oh, hi,' she said.

'Is something wrong?' he asked.

She knew she was probably showing signs of unhappiness. Most boys would take that as a signal to run and hide. Boys usually hated to hear girls' problems. She was surprised he'd asked about her obvious distress, and even more surprised that he was still there.

'I had an unexpected result from the Love Test,' she admitted.

'Yeah?'

'A couple who filled out the questionnaire showed every indication of being very well suited to each other, practically perfect. That's what the analysis showed. So I advised them to go ahead with the relationship.'

'What happened?'

'They went out on a date. But according to the girl who wrote to me, it was terrible. It doesn't make any sense, I don't understand.'

'I do,' Sean said.

Blair raised her eyebrows and spoke with just the slightest hint of sarcasm in her voice. 'You do? Then I wish you'd explain it to me.'

'You're treating love like a science,' Sean declared. 'It's not a science, it's magic.'

'Oh, *please*,' Blair said in disgust.

'No, really,' Sean insisted. 'That's why your questionnaire and your analysis won't work. No one can explain how or why love happens. It's a mystery, it's magic.'

'You're only looking at the superficial side of it,' Blair said. 'My questionnaire explores every aspect of the personality, every hobby and interest, all the likes and dislikes of each person.'

Sean shook his head. 'But that's got nothing to do with love. Sure, people can become friends if they both want to, I don't know, play golf or tennis or something. Or if they like the same band, or if they both like knock-knock jokes. But that's not the basis for love.'

'I *know* that,' Blair stated. 'But if you take all the elements into account—'

Sean didn't let her finish. 'You're still not accounting for the magic.'

Magic. Blair rolled her eyes. 'That's exactly what's *wrong* with most relationships. It's like, have you ever seen a magician pull a rabbit out of a hat?'

Sean nodded.

'Do you think there was actually a rabbit in that hat all the time?' she continued. 'No, of course not. Little kids might believe it, but everyone else knows it was just a trick, it wasn't real.'

'What's that got to do with love?' Sean asked.

'It's the same thing!' Blair declared. 'Maybe you meet someone, and you're snowed, or infatuated, or hung up, or whatever you want to call it. But it's just because of the way someone looks, or the mood you're in. It's not love, it's just a trick.'

'I don't agree with you,' Sean said, looking directly at her with something like sympathy in his blue eyes. 'I'm sorry, Blair, I don't mean to insult you, I just don't believe your questionnaire can work.'

Blair met his gaze. 'Yes, it can.'

'But it didn't.'

'There was a problem,' Blair admitted. 'I don't know what it is yet, but I'm going to examine the questionnaire and the analysis program and figure out what went wrong.'

'I don't think you're going to find an error in the program,' Sean said.

'We'll see about that,' replied Blair. Saying that, she meant to sound tough and determined. But at the same time, she knew she was smiling as she spoke.

When Andy arrived at the Double Click Café late on Sunday afternoon, he didn't see Jessica right away. He moved through the crowded main room, past the bar and looked into the other, smaller room. He spotted her at a station, but she had her back to him.

He wondered what she was doing. Was she in that chat room, telling her online pals that he was trying to be more romantic and attentive? And then going on to tell them them that his efforts had been futile?

He honestly had wanted to make last night a romantic evening. That had been his intention, that was why he'd suggested an evening alone instead of the basketball game. It just hadn't occurred to him that Jean-Claude van Damme and Sylvester Stallone were generally not featured in the type of movies that could be considered romantic. Those were the movies he'd wanted to see, and he hadn't even given her tastes any consideration.

Of course, on the other hand, he'd been more than a little put off when he saw those green peppers all over the pizza. Surely, by now, she should know how much he disliked green peppers. They'd eaten enough pizzas together. You would think she'd have noticed that every time they ordered the special pizza with everything he'd always ask the waiter to leave out the peppers.

No, last night probably couldn't be called a romantic evening. But then, Andy wasn't even quite sure what a romantic evening was supposed to be.

Jessica still hadn't turned around, and he decided not to disturb her. He couldn't yell across the room, not with all those other people working in there. And if she *was* complaining about him to her pals, she wouldn't appreciate having him come up behind her, with the possibility of him seeing what she was writing on the screen.

So he returned to the larger room, took a seat at a vacant station and logged on. He went into the newsgroup area and studied the list of groups he subscribed to, but for some reason none of them seemed very appealing that day. He didn't even feel like calling up the postings for Urban. If there were more flames from that idiot Killer, it would only darken the crummy mood he was already in.

Maybe he should look into something else, something that would distract him from his own problems. He could check into the international news headlines, and read about wars and natural disasters and all the other generally depressing stuff. That should make him stop fretting over his relationship with Jessica.

He'd just pointed the cursor towards the appropriate icon, a little picture of a newspaper, when a sharp cry distracted him. A guy at a station was gaping at his screen, and his face was turning red.

'What the hell—?' he yelled.

Greg came out from behind the bar and hurried over to him. 'What's the problem?'

'Look at this message on my e-mail!' the guy bellowed. By now, everyone in the room had stopped whatever they were doing and were looking at him. 'No, don't bother, I'll read it out loud. *Sir: Your threats towards the White House and the President of the United States have been duly received and noted. We must now inform you that you are currently under the constant surveillance of the Central Intelligence Agency, the Federal Bureau of Investigation, the armed forces of the United States and the Secret Service.*

Greg shook his head in bewilderment. 'Threats towards the White House?'

Then, from the other side of the room, came the all too familiar hysterical laugh of Paul Reedy. And Andy recalled that this was the same guy Paul had been hassling just a few days before.

The guy must have realised this, too. He leapt out of his chair and headed towards Paul with fury on his face and a clenched fist. Paul took one look at him, stopped laughing, and froze.

Greg was quick, and managed to pull the guy away before his fist could meet Paul's face. 'Take it easy!' he ordered the guy. 'Go sit at the bar and cool off!'

The guy continued to stare grimly at Paul, but he didn't struggle to remove himself from Greg's grip. He took a couple of deep breaths and slowly, his face began to return to a normal colour.

'Yeah,' he muttered. 'OK.' Greg let him go, and after one last withering look in Paul's direction, he turned and went to the bar.

Now Greg gave his full attention to Paul. 'Did you send that e-mail?' he demanded to know.

'What's everyone getting so uptight about?' Paul asked. 'Doesn't anyone around here have a sense of humour?'

'This is not a laughing matter,' Greg declared firmly. 'This is just as bad as making obscene phone calls or sending threatening letters by regular mail.'

Paul snickered. 'Whoa, buddy, don't go crazy here, it wasn't exactly pornography.'

Greg ignored that. 'You've been warned again and again about fooling around in here and using the Internet for practical jokes. Well, you've had your last warning. I want you out of here.'

'Hey, man, you can't tell me what to do,' Paul protested. 'It's a free country, remember the Constitution? I have my rights.'

'But this is not a free establishment, and as far as I'm concerned, you have no rights in here at all,' Greg responded. 'Now, are you going to leave on your own or am I going to have to throw you out?'

Paul attempted one more snicker. Then, he must have finally become aware that everyone in the café was watching him, and that no one was appreciating his joke. For a moment, he actually seemed a little nervous.

The room was utterly silent. Looking round, Andy had a feeling that all the others at the computer stations shared the same feelings he himself had. Paul Reedy had been a constant nuisance, and there couldn't be one person in the place who would mind at all if he was permanently banned from the Double Click Café.

Paul flushed. For a brief second, Andy almost felt sorry for the guy. Personal public humiliation wasn't anyone's idea of fun. Without another word, he turned and walked out of the café.

A couple of people started applauding, but Greg, still looking distressed, shook his head at them and went back to the bar.

'Excitement's over, folks,' he said, and everyone turned back to their computers.

Andy hadn't found any of this particularly exciting, just depressing. He had no interest now in becoming even more depressed by catching up on the world news.

He went back to the newsgroups, and clicked on to the advice group. Maybe somebody was offering him more tips on how to be romantic with Jessica.

There *was* another message. He accessed it, and saw that it was from Chris1492 again.

Have you ever thought of sending your girlfriend flowers?

Silently, Andy answered the question. No, he hadn't. But once again, he thought it was worth considering. Chris1492 seemed to know what he was talking about.

Chapter Six

For her junior year, Jessica had been lucky with her homeroom assignment. The past couple of years, she'd been stuck in homerooms with super-strict teachers. There would be the morning ritual that took place in every homeroom – attendance would be taken, and then there would be the usual announcements over the intercom.

But after that, the homeroom teachers Jessica had suffered in the past made the class go completely silent and study. These were the kind of teachers who thought homeroom should be treated as a class, and not as a period for catching up with friends, gossip, and general discussion of the past twenty-four hours. Or, in the case of a Monday, like today, a report on the weekend.

But this year, Jessica had been assigned to homeroom in the media centre, where the librarian, Mrs Annunziata, was nice and easy-going. After the attendance and the announcements, she let them hang out and relax.

'Just keep it down to a dull roar,' she would say, and they could talk and move about.

But on this particular Monday, when a stranger carrying a big plastic-wrapped bouquet walked into the media centre, all conversation and movement came to a complete halt. Everyone was watching as the man conferred quietly with Mrs Annunziata. Then she beckoned to Jessica.

Jessica, aware that all eyes were on her, came forward. 'Jessica Porter?' the man asked.

She nodded.

'Sign here please.' He handed a receipt pad to her, and Mrs Annunziata gave her a pen. She signed her name, and the bouquet was placed in her arms.

Immediately, a group of girls gathered round her, squealing.

'Jess! How absolutely gorgeous!'

'Yellow roses, wow!'

'Is it your birthday?'

'No,' Jessica said, looking at the bouquet with unconcealed delight.

'They're lovely, Jessica,' Mrs Annunziata said. She helped Jessica take the plastic off the flowers, and Jessica took a deep breath. It wasn't difficult at all, acting excited. But it was a lot harder to pretend she was surprised.

'Who are they from?' one of the girls asked.

'I don't know,' Jessica lied. She opened the little card that was attached to the plastic, and saw exactly what she expected to see. There were a dozen big yellow roses in the bouquet, surrounded by ferns and baby's breath, held together by a thick satin ribbon. This had to be pretty expensive, she thought.

But what was absolutely, utterly amazing was the fact that once again, he'd taken her advice. Well, the advice of Chris1492, that is.

Someone looking over her shoulder informed the others who the sender was. 'It says "Love, Andy". That's your boyfriend, isn't it?'

Jessica nodded, proudly.

'You're so lucky,' a girl moaned in envy. 'My boyfriend never sends me flowers.'

A couple of guys in the class didn't seem to be particularly thrilled about Jessica's flowers. They were giving each other meaningful looks, and Jessica knew what they were thinking. The word would get around, and other girls were going to expect flowers from their boyfriends.

'You need to put those in water,' Mrs Annunziata said. 'I'll find a vase. Your boyfriend is certainly romantic, Jessica.'

Romantic. Funny how that had never been a word she would use to describe Andy. Intelligent, yes, and witty, those were words she would use. Honest, kind, straight forward, and down to earth, definitely. But not romantic.

Actually, he'd probably never thought of her as a romantic type either. Jessica didn't even know if she'd call herself a romantic person.

But the flowers were glorious. And it was a lot of fun, being the centre of attention.

At that moment, with brilliant timing, Charlie Kingston walked into the media centre with a note from her homeroom teacher for Mrs Annunziata. She saw the flowers and looked questioningly at Jessica. Jessica grinned, and nodded. Charlie gave her a thumbs-up sign. She also raised her eyebrows as if she was asking Jessica what she would ask for next.

What else *could* she ask for, Jessica wondered. Could she get Andy to drop out of the debate team? That took up a lot of his time.

He did like debating a lot, though. Maybe that would be too selfish of her.

She could get him to change the way he dressed. She wasn't too crazy about the baggy jeans he wore so often, or the Urban tee-shirt he cherished.

She wondered what her chat line pals would have to say about all this. But she realised she didn't dare tell them. She'd like to think girls would always be loyal to each other, but she didn't really know any of those chat line people. Someone like SlyFox might be two-faced – her user name made Jessica uneasy. And SlyFox knew Andy's user name. She just might think it would be amusing to pass the news of Jessica's game on to him.

What would Andy do if he found out she was Chris1492? Just laugh, probably, and maybe even compliment her on her audacity.

Or maybe not. But she wasn't going to worry about that now.

During the last period that Monday, Blair's class had a pop quiz. She finished her test quickly, turned it in, and spent the rest of the time going over a print-out of the analysis program again.

She hadn't been able to identify an error on Sunday at the Double Click Café, and she'd stayed there till closing time. Today, she'd been so concerned that she spent her lunchtime in the school computer lab.

Eventually, she found one possible problem. It was something very minor, even inconsequential – a letter that she'd capitalised when it wasn't necessary. In her experience, capitalisation didn't usually affect programs, but computer science was still something new, and she didn't know everything.

She wished they'd got more advanced computer courses here at Briarcliff. Were there more courses at Lakeside High, she wondered. Maybe she could ask Sean the next time she saw him at the Double Click. After she told him she'd found the error in her program and corrected it, of course. And had more responses from her clients, too – responses that indicated how she'd been right about this all along.

She hadn't had any more replies yet from the couples she'd advised. She'd received four more completed questionnaires, though. But she hadn't sent any analysis back to them yet. She was uncertain about going ahead with that until she'd figured out what the problem was.

After class, she went to her locker. Andy was there, at his locker next to hers.

'Are you going to the Double Click Café?' Blair asked hopefully.

'Yeah,' he replied. 'I'm waiting for Jessica.' He seemed preoccupied.

She prompted him. 'Can I have a ride?'

'Yeah, sure.'

Jessica appeared just then, and Blair gasped. She was carrying a huge bouquet of yellow roses.

'Good grief, where did those come from?' she asked in amazement. 'What did you do, win a beauty contest or something?'

'They're from Andy,' Jessica said.

'Why?'

'No reason.'

Astonished, Blair looked at Andy. He had never struck her as the kind of boy who sent his girlfriend flowers for no particular reason. Andy looked strange – sort of pleased and sort of uncomfortable at the same time.

Jessica, too, was behaving oddly. 'You

should have seen the way people were looking at this in the cafeteria at lunchtime,' she said, gazing at Andy almost shyly.

'And looking at *us*,' Andy added, rolling his eyes. 'I've had to take a lot of teasing today.'

'Well, it was very, very sweet of you to do this,' Jessica said. 'Very romantic.'

Andy gave her a half-smile and shrugged.

It all made no sense at all to Blair. Boys were mysterious creatures, she decided.

When they arrived, it was clear that the Double Click Café had become more and more popular. Jessica and Andy got places, but Blair wasn't as quick. For the first time, she had to wait for an available computer.

She sat at the bar and ordered a soda from Hilary. Determined to grab the first empty seat, her eyes darted round the room. When she saw Sean come in, she wasn't sure how to react. Smile, or watch out that he didn't get a place before she did.

He wasn't alone this time. There was another boy, a little shorter and thinner, with him.

Sean spotted her at the bar. Grinning he came over with his companion. 'The place is packed today,' he commented.

'Yes,' she said, her eyes still scanning the room.

Again, he seemed to know what she was thinking, and he laughed. 'Don't worry, you were here first, I won't try to grab a seat out from under you.'

She had to laugh, too. 'Oh, I know you wouldn't do anything like that.'

'Did you figure out what went wrong with your questionnaire?' he asked her.

'I think so,' she replied.

The other boy spoke. 'Hey, pal, don't you have any manners?'

'Oh, sorry,' Sean said. 'Richie, this is Blair. Blair, Richie.'

'Nice to meet you, Blair,' Richie said.

'Same here,' she said, and then she saw someone leaving a station. She jumped off the bar stool. 'Excuse me, I have to get that place.' She slid into the seat just as someone else had a hand on the chair. 'Sorry!' she sang out.

Sean and Richie joined her at the station. 'Wow, you're fast,' Richie said admiringly. 'You must be working on something important.'

'I have to check my e-mail,' she said, focusing on the screen. 'I'm doing a project.'

She logged on, entered her mail program, and clicked to begin the mail retrieval process. As she waited, she heard Sean behind her explaining the Love Test to Richie. She was mildly, and pleasantly, surprised to hear him describing the program accurately. He didn't even sound like he was making fun of her project at all.

She didn't know how to feel when she saw that she had an e-mail from a client. She rather wished Sean wasn't standing directly behind her. She didn't want him to be a witness to an unhappy participant.

But then she saw that after the sender's name, the subject read *Love Test, Thank you!* Apparently she hadn't had another failure.

She brought the message on to the screen and read it rapidly. Then she turned round to see Sean's reaction.

But neither Sean nor his friend Richie were looking over her shoulder at her screen. Obviously, they both knew their netiquette.

So she invited them to hear her message. 'Listen to this! *Dear Love Test, a million thank yous! When Matthew first asked me out, I told him no. I thought he was a little nerdy. Then he saw your ad about the Love Test online, and he talked me into taking it with him. According to your analysis, we were perfect for each other. So I said, OK, I'd go out with him one time. I had a fantastic time! Matthew is not the least bit nerdy at all, he's great, but I would never have known that if I hadn't taken the Love Test.'*

When she'd finished reading the message, she turned and looked at Sean with pride.

'What do you think of that?' she asked triumphantly.

'She sounds happy,' Sean said.

Blair nodded. 'And she might never have connected with this guy if it wasn't for my Love Test.'

'You had good luck this time,' Sean remarked.

'It's got nothing to do with luck,' Blair argued. 'This is logic! It's science! The questionnaire provided the data that proved they were suited to each other.'

'I don't agree,' Sean replied calmly. 'I think it was just a coincidence.'

'No, you're wrong, it wasn't just a coincidence,' Blair stated stubbornly.

'Then how do you explain the couple who didn't work out?' Sean asked.

Blair considered that. 'All real scientists have to allow for some degree of error. Nothing is one hundred percent accurate.'

Richie piped up. 'She's right, you know. You can't say the project is a failure based on one report.'

Blair smiled brightly at him, grateful for this unexpected support.

'But you can't say it's a success based on one report either,' Sean countered. 'Come on, Richie, do you honestly think a computer can determine whether or not a relationship can work out?'

'It's possible,' he said.

'Would *you* trust a computer to make decisions about your love life?' Sean asked.

'Maybe,' Richie said, and he grinned. 'If I *had* a love life, that is.'

Blair turned to him eagerly. 'There must be someone you're interested in, someone you'd like to try this out with.'

Richie considered this. 'Not really... Hey, how about you?'

'How about me what?'

'Why don't you and I take the questionnaire and see what the analysis says?'

She glanced at Sean. He was frowning slightly.

'OK,' she said. 'Let's try it.'

'You're on,' Richie replied.

Blair told him how to access the questionnaire, and Richie agreed to do it right away.

'You're both nuts,' Sean muttered.

'We'll see about that,' Blair said, and she meant it too. For all she knew, Richie could turn out to be the great romance of her life. She wouldn't have guessed it – but that was what the Love Test was all about. No more guessing.

People were leaving and spaces were opening up in the main room now, so Andy went to the doorway leading into the other room and beckoned to Jessica. She glanced at him and smiled briefly, but she made no move to join him and continued to work at her station.

What was she doing now, Andy wondered. She was off in the other room, so he couldn't even see her. Was she still complaining to the girls on the chat line? The thought made him grimace. What did she have to complain about now? He'd given her compliments, he'd sent her flowers... He was lucky to have a mother who was sympathetic to romance, and let him use her credit card to order the roses.

She definitely seemed happy about the flowers. But then, if she was happy now, why was she off by herself, and not sharing an online experience with him? Why wasn't she there to hear how distressed he was about all this stupid flaming on his favourite newsgroup?

There were more flames today, and they were even worse than before.

Hey, you sleazy cruds! Did your mothers have any normal children?

Guess what, I'm starting an Anti-Urban group. We're going to boycott record stores that carry their music, we're going to burn their tapes and CDs!

The Anti-Urban group rules! We're going to plant bombs in the arenas where they perform!

They were all sent from Killer. Whoever he was, his attitude was getting sicker, Andy thought. He really wanted a reaction. And now, unfortunately, he was getting it. More members of the newsgroup were responding.

Beat it, scumbag!
Drop dead, Killer!
You're sick, man, get some help!
Go bother some other group!

Andy knew that Killer already *was* bothering other groups. When he checked into the relationship advice group, he selected some threads at random and found Killer's flames in several places. The comments were very weird. In the thread that dealt with a bossy sister, he suggested that the sender cut up her clothes. In another thread, where someone was fretting about their home life, he advised the person to run away from home and live on the streets.

The whole thing was really getting him down. He didn't find the crazy comments scary – just pathetic and pitiful and a nuisance.

He checked his own A Problem with my Girlfriend thread. Other people had posted their problems, so much of the advice offered had nothing to do with him. But there *was* another message from Chris1492. Whoever he was, he was certainly taking an interest in his relationship with Jessica.

If you really want your girlfriend to think

*you're becoming more romantic, take her
out for a date that's completely different from
what you usually do. Make it a surprise, an
evening of glamour. Tell her to dress up, but
don't tell her why. Pick her up in a limousine
with a chauffeur. Take her to La Maison
Rouge for dinner and dancing. Be sure to
make reservations in advance, and say that
you want candles and flowers on the table.
Wear a tuxedo. Order a bottle of champagne.
Tip the band so they will play your favourite
song and dance with your girlfriend. I
guarantee you, she will absolutely love this,
and she will think you are the most romantic
guy in the world.*

Andy read the long message twice, both
times in utter disbelief that verged on
shock. A rented limo, champagne, a French
restaurant – what kind of a world did
Chris1492 live in? Obviously, not the kind
of world where people lived on a meagre
allowance and a few extra dollars made by
typing up other people's term papers.

He knew his mother wasn't all *that*
romantic – he'd never be able to ask her for
the kind of money an evening like this
would cost.

Of course, he did have that cheque his
grandparents had sent for his last birthday.

Two hundred dollars. He hadn't even cashed it yet – he'd been holding on to it, until he decided what he wanted to spend it on. Maybe a real leather jacket.

He wasn't sure if two hundred dollars would be enough for a limo and a fancy dinner and all that. And was it even worth it? Would Jessica really like doing something like that? He never thought of her as the limousine type. It seemed to him that she'd been very happy going on picnics in the park.

As for dancing... he'd never been much of a dancer, and he definitely didn't enjoy it. At the last school dance, he and Jessica had a minor squabble over that, because she loved to dance. In fact, he'd been thinking about trying to improve, in time for the junior prom. Maybe get his sister to give him some lessons. But at the moment his sister was away at her university and wouldn't be coming home for at least another month.

La Maison Rouge... he'd heard of it, of course. His parents had gone there on their last wedding anniversary. It was the fanciest and most expensive restaurant in town.

Then he frowned. How did Chris1492

know about La Maison Rouge? This wasn't a local newsgroup, the subscribers were from all over the United States, and beyond. And La Maison Rouge wasn't a chain restaurant, like McDonalds, with establishments all over the world. How would Chris1492 know that this was the most expensive restaurant in the medium-sized suburban town where Andy was living? Was there something in Andy's original message that indicated his location? He didn't think so.

Then maybe Chris1492 was someone he knew, someone who also knew that Jessica wanted him to be more romantic. Blair? No, she was too practical. He didn't think her friend Caryn was into computers at all.

Could this be coming from Paul Reedy, as another stupid joke? No, Paul wasn't even allowed into the Double Click Café any more.

Maybe La Maison Rouge was even more famous than he thought. Or maybe it *was* a chain restaurant, all over the world. Just like Burger King – only a lot more expensive.

Chapter Seven

On Thursday evening at seven o'clock, Jessica stood in front of the mirror in her bedroom and wondered who she was looking at. She was only certain that this reflection couldn't be the same Jessica Porter she was accustomed to looking at in this same mirror every day. The reflection that confronted her was a total stranger.

She wasn't even wearing Jessica Porter's clothes. The navy-blue silk dress had been borrowed from Caryn, who had bought it for her cousin's bar mitzvah last spring. Jessica had nothing like this in her own wardrobe.

'You're welcome to it,' Caryn had said. 'When will I ever get to wear something this dressy again?'

It was definitely dressy, there was no doubt about it, and Jessica had never thought she'd be needing something like this to wear. It was very elegant, though a little stiff and uncomfortable. She also knew she'd be in fear all night that the strapless top would fall down, since she didn't have much to hold it up.

The high-heeled shoes on her feet hadn't been worn since her aunt's wedding six months ago. She had a feeling that her feet must have grown since then, and hoped the slight pinching in her toes wouldn't bother her too much later on. And what if her mother's necklace broke, and sent pearls flying all over the place?

She touched her hair, now stiff with spray and hard as a rock, and realised that it was giving her something else to worry about. If the French braid came undone, her hair would stick out all over the place, and she'd look like a witch.

Calm down, she ordered herself. Stop worrying. This is supposed to be fun, remember? And don't forget – it was all your own idea.

She was still in a state of semi-shock that Andy had gone for it. Of course, she didn't know for sure if he was going to follow *all* the advice of Chris1492. Andy had only told her to dress up and prepare for a big night.

But she had told Caryn and Blair that she thought he might be taking her to La Maison Rouge. They were both stunned.

'What happened, did he win the lottery or something?' Caryn asked.

And Blair had been very disapproving. 'My father won't even take my mother there, he says it's a rip-off.'

Her own parents had been pretty shocked, too. 'Where did Andy get that kind of money?' her father had asked. 'He's not dealing in drugs or anything like that, is he?'

Where *was* Andy getting the money for this, she wondered. That was something she hadn't taken into account when she'd designed the elegant date. Well, she wasn't going to worry about it now. Andy wasn't the wild spendthrift type, he was careful and practical. He wouldn't get into debt for her.

Or would he? Was he so absolutely crazy about her that he'd beg, borrow or steal to make her happy? The very notion gave her a little thrill. Though she wouldn't really want him to steal for her. He couldn't behave like much of a boyfriend if he was in jail.

At precisely seven thirty, the doorbell rang. Opening it, she got a brief glimpse of a limousine waiting at the kerb. But that wasn't what made her gasp.

'Andy! You look so—so—' She couldn't come up with the right word. She'd had no idea a tuxedo could change someone's appearance so dramatically.

'Yeah, that's what the guy at Formal Rentals told me,' Andy declared. 'He said my girlfriend wouldn't even recognise me, she'd be so impressed.'

Jessica wasn't sure if 'impressed' was the word she'd been searching for. Actually, she was fighting back a tremendous urge to giggle. Maybe she'd be impressed if the tuxedo actually *fitted* him. But poor Andy looked like a little kid wearing his father's clothes.

She felt a prick of guilt at her thoughts. Andy couldn't be very comfortable. He was a jeans and flannel shirt kind of guy, this just wasn't his style. And he kept running a finger around the inside of his collar and grimacing.

They left the house and stepping down from the porch, she let out what she hoped was a convincing shriek. 'Oh my goodness – Andy, that limo's for *us*?'

'Yep.'

Jessica found herself hoping that none of her neighbours were looking out of their windows at that moment. It was an immensely, obscenely long white stretch limo. A bored-looking man in a wrinkled uniform was standing by the car door and as they approached the car, he opened it for them.

The back seat was huge. Jessica shimmied over to one end, hoping her dress wasn't wrinkling too much, while Andy stayed at the other end. The driver got in and they took off.

Andy shifted around in his seat. 'This is weird, riding in a back seat,' he said. 'I feel like a child.'

'*I* feel like a princess,' Jessica assured him.

'That's because you *are* a princess,' he said, gallantly. 'At least you deserve to be treated like one.'

'Andy!' Jessica's eyes were wide with wonder. Where had he learned to speak like that? Not from Chris1492, she was sure of that. Maybe he'd found a new Web site – How to Talk to your Girlfriend.

She'd never ridden in a limousine before, so she took the opportunity to look around. It was like a hotel room, with a telephone and a bar and even a tiny television. There were buttons all over the place.

'I wonder what these buttons are for,' Andy murmured. He pressed one and above them, a sunroof opened and a blast of air hit the top of Jessica's head. She could feel the French braid unravelling.

'Andy, close it!' she screamed, trying to hold the braid together with both hands. But now Andy couldn't figure out which button he'd pressed. Frantically, he began pressing buttons at random. Music flooded the car, windows opened and closed, the television began to emit a strange buzzing sound, and a cabinet opened, revealing a wide selection of whiskeys. Thankfully, La Maison Rouge was only ten minutes away.

Jessica was still holding her hair in place when they arrived at the restaurant. She was so befuddled she didn't even remember to gasp when she saw where they were eating.

'Geez,' Andy complained. 'You act like you eat in places like this every day.'

'I'm too stunned to speak,' she managed to say.

They were greeted at the door by an elegant man who bowed. *'Bonsoir, monsieur, mademoiselle,'* he said. *'Bienvenue à La Maison Rouge.'*

Jessica took Spanish, not French, but she figured this was some sort of greeting so she smiled and nodded and tried to look like she was accustomed to being greeted in French. Fortunately he switched to English.

'Your table is ready,' he said, as they followed him across the room. When they arrived at their table, she saw that Andy had followed Chris1492's instructions completely. 'Oh, Andy,' she gasped. 'Flowers! And candles!'

'They cost extra,' Andy informed her proudly.

'May I bring you an aperitif?' the man asked.

Andy looked at Jessica questioningly. She had no idea what an aperitif was, so she didn't know whether or not she wanted the man to bring her one.

'OK,' Andy said to the man.

The man waited. After a moment he said, 'What may I bring you to drink, monsieur?'

Andy hesitated, and then, in an uncertain voice, he said, 'Champagne?'

The man smiled kindly. 'May I see some form of identification, monsieur?'

Andy looked like he wanted a hole to appear in the floor so he could sink through it. 'Um, well...'

Jessica felt awful. Quickly, she broke in. 'Actually, I don't really like champagne,

Andy. Maybe we could get some of that apple cider with bubbles instead?'

The man bowed his head in her direction. 'Very good, mademoiselle,' he said, and placed huge menus in front of them on their plates. They opened them up.

Jessica tried to read the items on the menu, but they were all in French, and she had no idea what most of the things were. But she *did* understand the prices and they made her eyes grow huge.

'What are *crevettes*?' Andy asked her, pointing to an item on the menu.

'I haven't the slightest idea,' Jessica confessed. 'Isn't that something you wear around your neck?'

'That's a cravat," said Andy.

'I was just kidding,' she said quickly. Jessica studied the French words and saw something called *ris de veau*. *Ris* had to mean rice, she figured. At least she'd recognise something on her plate.

'What are you getting?' she asked Andy.

'I guess I'll get a steak,' he said.

'Oh, Andy,' Jessica said. 'That's so American. This is a French restaurant.'

'Well, I'll get this steak *tartare* thing,' he said. 'That sounds French. What do you think that is?'

Jessica tried to sound like she knew what she was talking about. 'You know what tartar sauce is, Andy.'

'Oh, like you get with fish fingers,' he said. 'I never had it with steak. Well, I guess that might be good.'

The man reappeared with their fizzy apple juice. 'May I please take your orders, monsieur, mademoiselle?' he asked in a thick French accent.

They told the waiter what they wanted. When he left, Andy said, 'This isn't such a fancy place. He didn't even ask me how I wanted my steak cooked.' Then he mimicked the waiter. 'May I pleeze to tayke your ordairs?'

'Andy, it's not nice to make fun of someone's accent,' Jessica reprimanded him.

'Oh, come on, you don't think that's a real French accent, do you?' Andy asked. 'That guy's faking it.'

'He is not!' Jessica argued. 'They wouldn't have a fake French man in a real French restaurant.'

'Wanna bet?' Andy asked.

'What are we betting with?'

'Dessert?'

'You're on,' Jessica said. They reached across the table and shook hands. 'But how are we going to find out? Ask him for his passport?'

But now Andy was looking across the room, where a band had begun to play. Couples were leaving their tables to go out on to the dance floor. 'Excuse me,' he said, and got up.

Watching him approach the band, Jessica remembered that Chris1492 had advised him to tip the band to play a favourite song that he and his date could dance to. She was curious to see what he'd ask them to play. It wasn't as if the two of them had a special song.

When he returned to the table he was frowning.

'What's the matter?' she asked.

'They didn't know it.'

'They didn't know what?'

'The song I wanted them to play.'

She lowered her eyelids demurely. 'What song did you ask them to play, Andy?'

'*Gravity Sucks*. You know, by Urban.'

Her eyelids went back up. 'You can't dance to that song!'

He gave her an abashed smile. 'Jessica, I can't dance to any song.'

She sighed. Another element of her fantasy evening had just gone down the drain.

'Here comes our waiter,' Andy said. 'You gonna ask him for some identification or should I?'

But neither of them had the opportunity to ask the waiter anything. Just as he approached their table, he tripped. The tray he was holding soared out of his hands, and food went flying.

Jessica and Andy stared, their mouths hanging open as their table was sprayed with French sauce. What was even more amazing was the language that came out of the fallen waiter's mouth. Unless the French language contained the same four letter words that existed in English, Andy had won their bet!

An army of waiters surrounded the scene, and within seconds all evidence of the accident had disappeared. The man who had greeted Jessica and Andy at the door hurried over.

'*Excusez-moi*, I am so sorry!' he declared. 'Please, tell me your order. You are the guests of La Maison Rouge tonight.'

Andy brightened. 'You mean, we don't have to pay for our dinner?'

'That is correct,' the man said. 'Would you like to take another look at the menu?'

'I guess we'll just have what we ordered before,' Andy said, but Jessica broke in.

'Could you tell me what *ris de veau* is?'

'It is sweetbreads, mademoiselle.'

She frowned. 'What are sweetbreads?'

'It is a gland. The thymus gland.'

She felt sick. Then Andy spoke to the waiter. 'This steak tartare – it *is* steak, right?'

'Oui, monsieur. Raw steak.' The man smiled. 'Perhaps you would prefer something else. May I recommend the *steak hachis gratiné avec les pommes frites*? Would you like that instead?'

'We might,' Andy said. 'If we knew what it was.'

Jessica wasn't sure whether to die of embarrassment or kiss Andy in gratitude.

'Cheeseburgers with french fries,' the man said.

Andy looked at Jessica. She nodded.

'I hope we have better luck with dessert,' she said to Andy after the waiter left.

He grinned. 'Well, since you lost the bet... how about taking me to Häagen Dazs?'

She smiled back. 'You're on.' It might not be the most romantic food in the world, but at least they'd know what they were eating. And maybe a little caramel chocolate crunch could turn this evening into something less than a total failure.

Thursday night at the Double Click Café was busy and lively, even a little noisy. Normally, it would bother Blair, but tonight she really didn't have to concentrate. She knew exactly what she had to do, and it wasn't difficult. She had Richie's completed questionnaire and her own on a diskette. All she had to do now was feed it into the analysis program, print out the results, and inform Richie.

So, if it was so easy, why was she just sitting there at the station, staring into space, as if she was putting off some hugely difficult task? Did this have something to do with Richie himself?

She conjured up an image of Sean's friend. He semed to be nice. He wasn't bad looking. That was about all she could come up with to describe him. She didn't know much about his personality at all.

But that was what was so great about

the Love Test. She didn't *need* to know anything about him to decide whether she wanted to go out with him or not. The analysis would take care of that.

So why was she hesitating? What was making her put this off? If it was Sean who'd agreed to fill out the questionnaire, would she be dawdling like this?

But that was the point. She was attracted to Sean, that was for sure, but her goal was to disregard her instincts and work on making logical choices. Sure, it would be nice if Sean took the Love Test and it turned out that they were perfectly suited to each other. The fact that she was already attracted to him would be like icing on the cake.

But his wasn't Sean's questionnaire on the diskette she held in her hand. Sean would never fill out the questionnaire, he didn't believe in it. This was Richie's Love Test, and Richie might very well be someone with whom she could have a better relationship than she could have with anyone else – including Sean.

Without giving it any more thought, she uploaded the information from the diskette into the analysis program application. Then she waited. When a notation on the screen indicated that the process had been completed, she printed out the results. Then she sat back to examine them closely.

They were interesting, very interesting. According to the Love Test, she and Richie were an almost perfect match. Statistically, there was a ninety-two percent chance that they were destined for an enduring relationship.

And how did she feel about these results? She pressed her lips together, closed her eyes and gave her head a quick shake, as if she could somehow shake that question from her head. What did it matter how she felt? Feelings had nothing to do with this.

She rose and went over to the bar. 'Greg, can I use the telephone?'

Slumped over at the Double Click bar, Andy was actually glad that Jessica had an ice-skating lesson that Friday afternoon, and couldn't be with him here. He was too exhausted to make conversation.

'Rough day?' Greg asked.

'Rough night,' Andy replied.

He smiled sympathetically. 'Up late studying for an exam, huh? Or finishing a term paper? I remember what it was like, pulling an all-nighter.'

'Actually, I wasn't up studying,' Andy confessed to him. 'I took Jessica, my girlfriend, out for dinner and dancing at La Maison Rouge.'

Greg's eyebrows shot up and he whistled. 'Wow! What was it, her birthday?'

'No,' Andy replied. 'I just wanted to do something romantic.'

'La Maison Rouge,' Greg repeated. 'That's seriously romantic. And pretty expensive, isn't it?'

Andy grinned. 'Actually, we lucked out.' He told Greg about the accident in the restaurant. 'So all I had to pay for was the tuxedo rental and the limo.' He sighed. 'But that was still a hefty chunk of money.'

'Hilary and I have an understanding,' Greg said with a grin. 'No wild extravagances till we start making a decent profit.'

'Lucky you,' Andy said. 'I guess Hilary doesn't care if you're romantic or not.'

'Are you kidding?' Greg laughed. 'Hilary loves romantic stuff! I'm just lucky that romance doesn't have to cost a lot of money.'

'Not according to Chris1492,' Andy commented.

'Who's Chris1492?'

'Some guy in a newsgroup about relationships. I asked for some advice on how to make my girlfriend happy.'

'This Chris1492 – what makes him such an authority?' Greg asked. 'Or her?'

'Her?'

'He could be a girl.'

'Yeah, I guess so,' Andy said, and once again he wondered about the advice to go to La Maison Rouge. Could Chris1492 be a girlfriend of Jessica's, someone who actually knew what Jessica wanted?

'Are you going to keep on taking this person's advice?' Greg asked.

'I don't think I can afford to,' Andy replied. 'But I don't know what else to do.'

'Why do you have to do anything?' Greg asked. 'If you have to buy her love, what kind of relationship is it? Excuse me, Andy, I see someone needing some help.' He left the bar, but his words remained behind.

'If you have to buy her love… ' Was that what he was doing?

Greg was right. What else could it be called? And why did he think he needed to do that? He knew the sort of person Jessica was. She wasn't the kind of girl who sold her affection to the highest bidder.

It wasn't working anyway. Chris1492 didn't know what he was talking about. Andy could tell that Jessica wasn't really having any fun last night, any more than he was having fun, and she was no happier than he was. Whatever was wrong with their relationship, all the expensive romantic gestures in the world weren't going to fix it. Flowers and dinners were no more effective than Blair's dumb Love Test could be. None of this had anything to do with real feelings.

He went to a computer station, logged on, and clicked directly into the relationship advice group. There were no postings from Chris1492, but Andy went ahead and addressed him in a message.

To: Chris1492, whoever you are. From: Andy513. I appreciate the advice you've been giving me, but you can stop giving it now. It's not working. I think that maybe you know Jessica, and you think that this is what she wants. But you don't know her like I do. She can't be made happy with flowers and dinners and all the other things that money can buy. She isn't that kind of girl. I don't know how to fix our relationship. Maybe it can't be fixed. But I do know that real love can't be bought.

He clicked on Send Message and hoped Chris1492 would check the newsgroup before sending him any more advice.

Now he wanted to get his mind off this, and he was even willing to subject himself to Killer to do it. He clicked into the Urban newsgroup and braced himself.

There were more flames. Killer was bragging that he'd been shoplifting Urban compact discs from record stores. He said he was spreading rumours on the Internet that Urban's band members were communicating secret satanic messages in their music, and encouraging young kids to try drugs.

There were more counter-attacks, too, from the newsgroup subscribers, pleading with Killer to go away, threatening him with bodily harm if they ever found out who he was.

In all the postings, there wasn't one that had anything to do with the band itself or its music. There was no evidence of the kind of intelligent discussions that Andy had enjoyed in the group. Killer had ruined it.

Then he noticed something at the top of his screen. On the little mailbox icon, the flag was up, indicating that someone had sent him an e-mail. He clicked on the icon.

It was a letter from one of the Urban subscribers, and it appeared to have been sent out to numerous members of the group.

Dear Urbanites: Are you sick of Killer? Do you want to get our old newsgroup back? I think we can do something about this. Did you read his flame about shoplifting? He mentions a particular store – Sunburst Record and Tapes.

The writer went on to say that Sunburst was a chain of record stores that only existed in a certain region. This meant that Killer had to be living in that region if he was hanging out in a Sunburst store. The writer asked that all Urban fans who lived in that region meet in an online relay chat room at two o'clock in the afternoon on Saturday, tomorrow. Together, they could try to come up with a plan to locate this creep and stop him from bothering them.

Andy read this with more than his usual interest. He knew Sunburst Record and Tapes – there was a Sunburst store in the mall only ten minutes from his own home. He made a mental note to meet the others online tomorrow.

It was Friday night and Blair stood in front of a restaurant, Tonio's Cucina, and waited for Richie to arrive for their agreed date. She remembered that, according to the questionnaires they'd completed, both she and Richie put a high degree of importance on punctuality. And according to her watch, it was now precisely seven o'clock, the time they'd decided to meet for their date.

She frowned. But then, as she glanced through the window into the restaurant, she saw a clock on the wall. It said exactly two minutes before seven o'clock. She had to admit there was a possibility her watch could be a little fast.

But her questionnaire was accurate. Within the next sixty seconds, Richie showed up.

They greeted each other and went inside the restaurant. Richie gazed appreciatively at the colourful checked tablecloths and the candles dripping down fat wine bottles that stood on each table.

'I've never been here before,' he said, 'but I like this kind of place. It's nicer than a fast food place, but more casual than a fancy restaurant.'

Blair nodded complacently. 'I knew you'd like it. It's one of my favourite places.'

They sat down and a waiter brought them menus. As Richie studied his, Blair said, 'I'll bet I know what you want – eggplant parmigiana.'

Richie gasped. 'How did you guess?'

'Because that's what I want,' she said. 'Remember, we're ninety-five percent compatible. It's only logical that we'll like the same things.'

'Oh, yeah, that's right,' he said. 'Actually, to tell you the truth, I haven't decided between the eggplant parmigiana or the cheese ravioli. That's one of my other favourite things to eat.'

'Mine, too,' Blair said, nodding.

'I have an idea,' Richie declared. 'Why don't you get the eggplant parmigiana and I'll get the cheese ravioli and we can share.'

Blair smiled approvingly. 'Excellent.' She'd been on the verge of suggesting this herself.

They both ordered salads, and they both stipulated 'no onions, please' to the waiter. Blair thought this was a good sign too. Not only did she hate the taste of onions, she didn't like the smell of them near her. Wait till Sean heard how well this was going.

Now that the waiter had disappeared, they faced each other across the table. 'This is kind of weird,' Richie said.

'How do you mean?' asked Blair.

'Well, when I go out with someone for the first time, this is when you start asking questions and get to know each other. But if we're so perfectly suited, there's not much to find out, is there? I mean, we probably like all the same things.'

Blair nodded in agreement. 'Like, if you could choose between getting a tiny, fast sports car or a big van, you'd choose the van, right?'

'Absolutely,' Richie said. 'You can go camping with a van. Would you pick the van?'

'Of course,' Blair replied. 'A van is much more practical, and it's safer, too.'

'How about this one?' Richie asked. 'Choose between a summer vacation at the beach or in the mountains.'

'Mountains,' Blair responded, automatically. 'I burn too easily at the beach.'

'Me too,' Richie said, 'and I'd rather go hiking than swimming.'

'So would I,' Blair agreed. 'I'll bet you'd rather play tennis than golf.'

They continued like this, and learnt that they had a huge amount in common – some of the same favourite books, movies and music too. They both preferred grapefruit juice to orange juice, maths classes to English classes, and jeans with a button fly, not jeans with a zipper.

They managed to discuss all these things within five minutes. For the next five minutes, it wasn't so easy. Blair felt that they'd covered nearly all the items in the questionnaire, and nothing was a surprise.

She couldn't deny it. She was *bored*. But was that the worst feeling in the world?

At least she knew, with reasonable certainty, that Richie could never break her heart.

Chapter Eight

Jessica practically collided with Andy when she walked into the Double Click on Friday evening.

'Hi!' she said.

'Hi!' he replied.

After a brief pause, she said, 'I didn't see you at school today.'

'No, I didn't come into the cafeteria at lunchtime,' he told her, but she noticed he didn't explain why.

Jessica nodded. 'That was fun, last night, at the restaurant.'

'Yeah, we lucked out,' he said.

And then there was another silence. What was wrong with him, she wondered. This was awful, she thought. This was absolutely awful.

'You look tired,' she said.

'I am,' said Andy. 'I'm going home now, and I think I'm going right to sleep.'

'That's a good idea,' she added lamely.

He went past her and opened the door. Then he turned back. 'I'll call you, tomorrow.'

'OK,' she said and he was gone.

She went over to a computer station and sat down. Now what, she wondered. Everything seemed OK last night. What could have changed between then and now?

She wished Chris1492 was a real person who could give *her* some advice. Maybe someone else in that group could. But how could she possibly ask for advice like that? Even if she changed her user name again, so Andy couldn't recognise it, he'd be able to recognise the situation she described.

She couldn't talk to her friends – Caryn would disapprove, and Blair would just go on nagging her to take that stupid Love Test with Andy. She couldn't talk to Charlie Kingston – Charlie wasn't that close a friend, and besides, Charlie would probably think she was making a fuss over nothing.

She decided to check into the advice newsgroup anyway. Reading about other people's problems might give her some ideas on how to deal with her own. She spotted a new thread that caused her eyes to widen – it was called *To: Chris1492*. She clicked on to it.

To: Chris1492, whoever you are… maybe you know Jessica and you think this is what she wants… She isn't that kind of girl…

There was another message too, from an unknown person who just happened to have read his message. It was brief and it got right to the point.

To: Andy513: She doesn't deserve you.

A sick feeling came over her, almost like a wave of nausea. And suddenly, she was so disgusted with herself that she wanted to die. Or, at least burst into tears.

She managed to refrain from doing either, but something must have given her feelings away, because Hilary appeared by her side.

'Jessica? Are you all right?'

Her brain ordered her to say yes, but instead her head twisted back and forth sideways, signalling no.

'Why don't you come on over to the bar and we can talk,' Hilary suggested.

Jessica obeyed. She didn't know why she was doing this, since she had absolutely no intention of confessing her sins to anyone or letting them know what a wretched, undeserving person she was. And yet, the minute she found herself sitting on the bar stool and facing Hilary, the whole ugly story came pouring out. So did the tears.

'I didn't mean it to go this far,' she wept.

'I just wanted our relationship to be better.'

Hilary nodded sympathetically.

'Pretty stupid way of going about it,' she went on, and waited for Hilary to offer consoling noises, to make her feel less guilt-stricken.

'Yeah, pretty stupid,' Hilary said. 'No, I take that back. *Very* stupid.'

Her brisk, matter-of-fact statement did a good job of stopping Jessica's flow of tears. 'I just wanted a little more attention,' she said.

'Did you think that would improve the relationship?' Hilary asked. 'Getting more attention?'

'I was willing to give him more attention, too,' Jessica replied in self-defence. 'That's why I came here in the first place, because he was so into this online stuff. No offence intended, but this really isn't my thing.'

Hilary smiled. 'No offence taken. I'm not completely wild about online communication myself.'

'You're not?'

'In some ways, it's fantastic,' Hilary said. 'People often find it easier to express themselves like this, and they'll open up more. But it can constrict communication, too. And there are dangers.'

'What do you mean?'

'Look at what you've just done,' Hilary said. 'That's typical of the problems people can get themselves into. You see, it's very tempting, and simple, to be more deceitful online than it is in real life. You're not making eye contact and nobody can see your face.'

Jessica couldn't remember anyone ever calling her deceitful before. It was an ugly word. But she couldn't argue about it, because she knew Hilary was right.

Hilary spoke more kindly now. 'You know, even people who would never lie directly to a friend can find themselves doing it online. It doesn't seem real, it's more like playing a game. It's just so easy, to hide behind a faceless user name and say anything you want to say. And not feel responsible for the consequences.'

Slowly, Jessica nodded. What Hilary was saying was exactly what she had done.

'What do I do now?' she murmured plaintively, staring down at the bar. 'Should I tell Andy everything?'

Hilary shrugged. 'That's for you to decide. Some people think confession is good for the soul, it makes a person feel less guilty. Me, I'm not so sure it's all that good for the person you're confessing to. Does it make that person feel any better?'

Jessica tried to imagine Andy's reaction on hearing the whole story. It made her shudder.

She looked up at Hilary. 'Maybe... maybe it would be better just to stop lying, huh?'

'Maybe,' Hilary said. 'Of course, then you still have your original problem – making your relationship better. How are you going to do that?'

Jessica thought Hilary already knew the answer and she took a stab at answering it herself. 'By talking?'

Hilary smiled. 'There's nothing like good old-fashioned, face to face, low tech communication.'

A group of people had just come into the café and they were looking around. 'Excuse me, Jessica,' Hilary said. 'They look like newcomers.'

She came out from behind the bar to speak to them. Jessica got off the bar stool and went back to her computer station. She was still in the relationship advice newsgroup.

She clicked on 'send new message' and entitled it *To: Andy513.*

OK, I won't give you any more advice.

Actually, I don't have any more to give. In a way, you were right. I thought I knew your girlfriend. I told you to do what I thought would make her happy. But I was wrong. I don't know her at all. So just forget everything I wrote to you.

Did you see your other message? Maybe that person is right. She just doesn't deserve you.

Blair had no e-mail waiting for her to read on Saturday morning at the Double Click Café. There weren't any Love Tests being submitted, and there were no more reports on the questionnaires she'd already responded to. She leaned back in her chair, looked up at the ceiling, and wondered what to do next.

'Looking for heavenly advice?' asked a voice from behind her.

She turned around and faced Sean. 'Oh, hi.'

'Hi,' he said. 'How's the love business going?'

'OK,' she said. Then, afraid she didn't sound sufficiently enthusiastic, she added, 'Good.'

'Are you speaking for yourself?' he asked her.

'What do you mean?'

He got to the point. 'How was your date with Richie last night?'

'Not that it's any of your business,' Blair said coolly. 'But it was fine.'

'I knew you were going to say that,' he said.

'How? Are you a mind reader?'

'No, I'm just a sensitive guy,' he said with a smile. 'In fact, I took a test for sensitivity once, and I got the highest marks.'

'Congratulations!' she said sarcastically.

'OK, I'll tell you the truth. I talked to Richie on the phone this morning and I asked him the same question.'

Blair nodded, and tried not to sound too curious when she asked, 'What did he say?'

'The same thing you just said. Fine.'

'Well,' Blair said complacently, 'that makes sense, doesn't it?'

Sean pulled a chair over from the next station and sat down, facing her. 'Are you in love?'

She was taken aback by his bluntness, and she stalled for time. 'What?'

'Are you in love?' he asked again. 'With Richie?'

'In love?' she repeated. 'That's a pretty strong word. I mean, we've only had one date.'

'But isn't that the whole point of your Love Test?' Sean pressed. 'You don't *need* a dozen dates to find out if you're in love.'

Blair fumbled for the right words. 'Well, yes, but, like I said before, there's always a margin of error you have to take into consideration. What the questionnaires prove is that the *probability* of love exists. I might not be able to say I'm in love with Richie right this minute, but in time I'm sure I could be.'

'That's not what *he* says,' Sean told her.

She knew he was trying to provoke her and she wanted to end this conversation right now. But curiosity got the better of her.

'Oh, really? What does he say?'

'He likes you,' Sean said. 'He thinks you're an interesting person. He thinks you have a lot in common, and that he would enjoy doing things with you. Like playing tennis, or hiking in the mountains.'

'So? What's wrong with that?'

Sean studied her face seriously. 'He wants to be *friends* with you, Blair. Just friends. That's all.'

She fell silent, as she tried to figure out how to respond to this. He misinterpreted the silence, and his expression changed.

'I've hurt your feelings,' he said suddenly. 'I didn't mean to do that. I'm sorry, honestly, I'm very sorry.'

'That's OK,' she replied automatically.

'I guess maybe I'm not as sensitive as I think I am,' he declared.

He really did look ashamed.

'That's OK,' she said again. 'Don't feel bad. You didn't hurt my feelings.'

He grinned. 'I didn't think so.'

The sudden change in tone startled her. 'What?'

'I knew you weren't hurt.'

She raised her eyebrows. 'Oh, really?' she asked in a haughty tone. 'I beg your pardon? How could you possibly know what I'm feeling? And don't you dare tell me it's your natural sensitivity.'

'Just a wild guess,' he replied. 'Or maybe it's common sense. You two have a lot in common, but you're not in love with him. So it wouldn't hurt your feelings to know he's not in love with you.'

His logic was annoying. 'I'm sure that if Richie and I really tried to establish a relationship, something could come of it,' she declared.

'But what would be the point?' he asked. 'If you don't have strong feelings for him naturally, why should you try to force yourself to have them? And if you don't have the feelings now, what makes you think they can come later?'

It was on the tip of her tongue to say something like 'feelings have nothing to do with it', but she realised how stupid that would sound. After all, they were talking about love.

As she contemplated her next retort, he spoke again.

'Would you go out with me?'

She wasn't sure she heard correctly. 'What?'

'Is your hearing all right? You've been saying "what?" a lot today.'

She stared at him without replying.

'OK,' he said with a sigh. 'I'll repeat that. Would you go out with me?'

'On a date?' she asked stupidly.

'Yes, on a date. Tonight. There's a dance over at my school. Nothing formal or fancy, but they've got a real band and it's supposed to be good.'

There it was – that hollow feeling in the pit of her stomach. She couldn't speak.

'Look, I know it's the last minute,' Sean said. 'I know some girls would act all huffy and insulted and say they already had plans, even if they didn't. And maybe you really do have plans. But if you don't… well, I don't think you're the kind of person who has to play games.'

She still couldn't speak.

He gave an exasperated sigh. 'So, how about it? Do you want to go out with me?'

Her mind was spinning. Of course, she *wanted* to go out with him. She'd been wanting to go out with him ever since she first met him. Which was exactly why she wouldn't go out with him. Not unless—

'Will you fill out the questionnaire?' she asked.

'You want me to take the Love Test before we go out?'

She nodded. 'I'll compare it with mine, and if the results are positive–'

He wouldn't let her finish. 'No.'

Disappointment engulfed her. 'Why not?'

'You know why not. I don't believe in it. I don't believe in establishing a relationship based on a computer analysis.'

Blair had her response ready. 'Well, I don't believe in taking chances when someone could get hurt.'

'But that's always the risk,' said Sean.

'I like to avoid risks,' she replied.

He gazed at her steadily. 'That's too bad,'

he said, and he sounded as if he really meant it.

'Yes,' she echoed. 'Too bad.'

He got up. 'I'll see you, Blair.'

She watched him leave, and wondered how it was possible to have a broken heart when you hadn't even given the relationship a chance to start.

At precisely noon, Andy was logged on, following yesterday's instructions. He entered the keyword that would put him into a 'room' where the Urban fans were supposed to gather. The person who had sent the message yesterday took charge of the meeting.

Twister: *Something has to be done about this Killer. He's ruining our newsgroup.*

Frogman: *He's bothering other groups too. And he's sending nasty e-mails.*

Sam498: *But there's nothing we can do. Anyone can access a newsgroup. You can't stop him.*

LPN4: *Unless we hire a hitman to break his fingers*

Twister: *Exactly. That's my plan.*

Andy was startled, and he jumped into the discussion.

Andy513: *You're going to use violence?*

Twister: *If it's necessary. At least we can scare him.*

Frogman: *We could get into trouble sending threats over the Internet.*

Twister: *We're not going to send threats over the Internet. We're going to do it in person. Here's my plan.*

Andy read Twister's scheme with a horrified fascination. It seemed that Twister had already made contact with Killer, through an e-mail message, using the name MadDog. MadDog had told Killer that he'd read his postings and thought he was cool. He'd said he wanted to meet IRL with Killer, so they could plan some sort of wide-ranging nuisance activities on the Internet, and become famous as Net terrorists.

Twister: *I told him I know he lives in my region because he mentioned Sunburst Records. So I asked him to meet me today at three o'clock at the Chow Fun Chinese Restaurant, on Interstate 67, near the Pine Hill exit.*

Andy513: *What are you going to do to him?*

Twister: *I want everyone who lives within sixty miles of Chow Fun to meet there.*

There's a big parking lot out back. I'll get him to come outside, and we'll show him what happens when you flame a newsgroup. I'm counting on you guys. This is the only way we'll lose him.

Andy wanted to be there. He didn't plan on becoming a part of some sort of brawl, he wasn't into fighting, but he was thinking that it wouldn't necessarily come to that. Maybe a face-to-face confrontation would be sufficient to discourage Killer.

He looked at his watch. It was now twelve thirty. He knew the Chow Fun restaurant, his family had stopped there once on the way back from visiting his grandmother. It would take him at least forty-five minutes to get there, maybe longer if there were still roadworks in progress on the highway. He'd told his father he'd pick up some stuff at the hardware store and bring it home when he left the Double Click, and his father needed the stuff for this afternoon. He'd have to hurry if he was going to do that and make it to Chow Fun on time.

It was while he was hurrying out of the café that he realised he hadn't checked the advice newsgroup, to see if there was any response from Chris1492 to Andy's message yesterday. But he was in no rush to do that. At this point, he felt that he could only deal with one online problem at a time.

And dealing with Killer *had* to be easier than dealing with his love life.

Chapter Nine

It was just before one o'clock when Jessica walked into the Double Click. This had been a difficult decision – should she wait at home for Andy's promised call, or should she go to the café, in the hope that he was there?

She had decided to go to the café because she was sick of staring at the telephone and begging it to ring. She thought that, at the café, there would be more distraction – she could strike up a conversation with someone and it would help pass the time.

When she arrived, she wasn't so sure. There weren't many people there, and the ones who *were* there were huddled over their computers, oblivious to anyone else. But when she saw Blair sitting at the bar, she brightened. As she sat down on the stool next to hers and greeted her, she could sense that she wasn't in the mood for a chat.

'Have you seen Andy?' Jessica asked her.

'Huh?'

Jessica repeated her question.

'No. Oh, wait, yeah. He was here.' Blair looked around. 'I guess he left.'

'Did he say where he was going?'

'No.'

Blair looked so down that, for a moment, Jessica forgot her own problems. 'What's the matter?'

'I had a date last night. With my Love Test person, Richie. According to the questionnaires, we were an almost perfect match.'

'Oh.' Jessica gazed at her friend sympathetically. 'And it didn't work out, huh?'

'No, it went off fine,' Blair said. 'We got along great, we agreed on everything, he's a really nice person.'

'Then what's the problem?'

Blair sighed heavily. 'He's not in love with me.'

'Are you in love with him?'

'No.'

The conversation was beginning to give Jessica a headache. 'I don't get it. If you're not in love with him, why are you upset that he's not in love with you?'

'Because... because we *should* be in love. We're an almost perfect match! I'm willing to give it a chance, but he just wants to be friends.'

'Blair,' Jessica said kindly, 'you can't just make love happen if it's not there. Just because you and Richie agree about everything doesn't make you a perfect love match. Look at me and Andy.'

'What *about* you and Andy?' Blair asked pointedly. 'Are you guys getting along so great these days?'

Jessica didn't answer that.

Blair went on. 'Neither of you have been looking particularly happy lately. He didn't even come to meet you in the cafeteria on Friday, and he always does that.'

'We're having some problems,' Jessica admitted.

Blair sniffed. 'You two are *always* having problems. Like I said before, I've never known a couple who argue as much as you and Andy do.'

'But that wasn't a problem,' Jessica said suddenly.

Blair looked sceptical. 'Fighting isn't a problem?'

'It wasn't fighting, it was never fighting,' Jessica insisted. 'It was discussion. Anyway, lately, we haven't been arguing, or fighting like you call it. I thought we were both trying to be more like a normal couple. But it's now that things don't feel right.'

'That doesn't make sense,' Blair stated.

'I know,' Jessica said. 'But I guess love isn't supposed to make sense. And I don't think it has anything to do with liking the same movies.'

'Then what exactly is it?' Blair demanded to know.

'I haven't the slightest idea,' Jessica confessed. 'Magic, I guess.'

'Magic,' Blair scoffed.

Jessica smiled sadly. 'Think about it, Blair. Love is the subject of zillions of poems. But are there any mathematical formulas or science experiments dedicated to love?'

'There *should* be,' Blair stated sullenly.

'But there aren't,' said Jessica. 'And you're just going to have to live with that, Blair.'

Blair wasn't unhappy when Jessica left her to go online at a computer station. Her friend had done nothing to improve her mood.

She wasn't thinking about Richie any

more, she was thinking about Sean. But every time his face popped into her head, she tried to replace it with other faces – the faces of Denny, Tony, Eric, all the boys she'd been crazy about who had broken her heart. Never again, she kept telling herself. No more tears for me.

Then why did she feel on the verge of them right this very minute?

Jessica had been talking about the zillions of poems that had been written on the subject of love. Blair knew she was right, and at that moment she remembered a line from one of them – something like,

Tis better to have loved and lost,
Than never to have loved at all.

She couldn't remember the name of the poem or the poet who wrote it. But she did remember what she'd thought the first time she'd heard it – that this poet, whoever he or she was, had obviously never been dumped by anyone, like she had been.

She didn't want to give up on her mission, she wouldn't give up, not if there remained some chance of finding a love that wouldn't end in pain. Maybe if she went over the questionnaire again... maybe she needed more questions about personality rather than hobbies or interests.

She went back to a computer station, accessed the Love Test, and began to study it. She was concentrating so hard that she jumped when she heard someone behind her.

'Blair?'

She turned. 'Hi, Sean.'

He looked unusually serious. 'I've changed my mind.'

'What?'

'I'll fill out your questionnaire.'

She was more than surprised. 'You will? Really? You're not teasing me?'

He nodded, and then shook his head. 'Yes, I really will, and no, I'm not teasing you.'

She tried to hold back a triumphant smile, but she wasn't quite successful. 'Then you admit there's got to be something to this.'

He shrugged. 'I'm not going to lie to you, and tell you I believe in your Love Test. But I want to go out with you. I want to get to know you. And if this is the only way I can get you to go to the dance with me tonight, I'll do it.'

Blair had to remind him about something. 'If we don't get a positive score—'

He finished her sentence for her. 'You won't go out with me, I know. But at least this way I've got a chance.'

Blair was impressed. She had a pretty good feeling that Sean, like herself, was a strong-willed person. It couldn't be easy for him to agree to do something he didn't really approve of. But he was willing to do it, just for her. And there was that sensation in her stomach again...

'OK,' she said briskly. 'I've got the questionnaire on the screen right here. It shouldn't take you more than thirty minutes to answer everything. I'll be at the bar. Just send it to my e-mail address when you're done, and tell me. I'll put it through the analysis program right away, and we'll have the results in minutes.'

He smiled slightly. 'In time for you to go home and change for the dance?'

That smile, such a wonderful, natural, honest smile – stop it, she ordered herself. Get a grip on yourself.

'Yes,' she said coolly. 'If the result is good. If not, there'll be plenty of time for you to find another date.'

Andy arrived at the Chow Fun restaurant a

lot earlier than he'd expected. There'd been hardly any traffic, and the roadworks on the highway were finished. It was only one thirty when he walked in.

Chow Fun was a huge place that looked more like a factory than a restaurant, and it certainly wasn't the place a person would go to for a quiet, relaxing meal. But the Chinese food was good, and the service was fast. It was the kind of place where a person would stop to grab a quick bite while on the way to somewhere else. Waiters bustled, and people were coming and going all the time.

That was probably why Twister had chosen it for the place to gang up on Killer, Andy thought. Nobody would notice a group of guys hustling another guy out to the parking lot.

A waiter passed by with a plate of something that smelt delicious, and Andy realised that he was hungry. He sat down in a booth where he could watch the door. Not that he'd be able to recognise Killer, or Twister, or anyone else from the Urban newsgroup, but it would be interesting to guess at who they might be.

When a waiter came by, he ordered a couple of egg rolls and a bowl of won ton soup, and as he waited for his food, he looked around to see if he saw anyone who might be a member of his newsgroup or an obnoxious, nasty flamer. He saw families, he saw people with briefcases, there was a group of older ladies, some guys in tennis clothes – no one looked like a real possibility. Of course, it was still early.

His soup and egg rolls arrived within five minutes, and he'd just dipped his spoon into the soup when he recognised someone coming in the door. He ducked his head, practically burying his face in the soup. Paul Reedy was the last person he wanted to see today, at this time. He'd want to find out what Andy was doing there. Then he'd want to hang out and watch the attack on the flamer, all the while making stupid jokes with the Urban guys. It would be very embarrassing if they thought Paul was a friend of his.

When he thought he was safe, he looked up again. Bad move. Paul was looking straight at him. Andy steeled himself for one of Paul's raucous greetings.

But it didn't come. Paul was coming towards him, but he didn't look like he wanted to start horsing around.

'What are you doing here?' he asked Andy.

Andy gestured to the food on his table. 'Eating, what else?'

'Oh. Right.'

'Isn't that what you're going to do?'

Paul shook his head. 'I hate Chinese food.'

'Then why did you come here?' Andy asked. 'That's all they have.'

'I didn't know that,' Paul said.

This guy wasn't only a clown, he wasn't too bright, Andy thought. What other kind of food would you expect to find in a restaurant called Chow Fun?

He noticed that Paul kept looking at the door.

'You meeting someone?'

Paul nodded. He didn't move. And he didn't look very comfortable either.

Andy's naturally decent manners were stronger than his dislike for Paul. 'You want to sit down?' he asked, hoping the reluctance in his voice was clear.

It wasn't. Paul sat down opposite him and looked at Andy's plate.

'What are those?'

'Egg rolls,' Andy said. 'You want to try one?'

Paul shrugged. Andy cut an egg roll in half and handed it to him.

'Not bad,' Paul said. 'How are things at the Double Click Café?'

'OK,' Andy said. 'Same.' After a second, he added, 'You want to talk to Greg about coming back?'

Paul uttered a short, harsh laugh. 'Are you kidding? No way. I got better things to do than hang out with the slime-buckets in that place.'

'Oh, come on, Paul,' Andy remonstrated. 'There are some nice kids in there.'

'Computer nerds,' Paul said. 'They should get a real life. Wake up and smell the pizza.'

Andy's brow puckered. He'd heard that before. Where?

Paul was looking at the door again. 'Do you know what time it is?' he asked Andy.

Andy looked. 'Almost ten to two.'

And then, very slowly, like the light of the sun coming up on the horizon, the realisation dawned on him.

'It's you,' he whispered.

Paul looked at him sharply. 'What?'

'It's you! You've been posting the flames on the newsgroups!'

Paul's beady eyes were darting back and

forth. 'I don't know what you're talking about.'

'Yes you do,' Andy said. 'You're Killer. It was you all along!'

Paul rolled his eyes and made a scornful noise that wasn't very convincing.

'Why, Paul? Why have you been doing that?'

It appeared that Paul's instinctive desire for attention carried more weight than his desire to keep his online games a secret.

He actually had the gall to grin. 'I had you guys going, huh? Really made you crazy.'

Andy stared at him in bewilderment. 'But you're not answering my question. Why do it? What are you getting out of this?'

'Just a joke, man,' Paul said.

'It's not a funny joke,' Andy declared.

'That's your opinion.'

Andy thought about the Urbanites on their way to Chow Fun right that minute. 'No, that's not just my opinion.'

'You some sort of authority on what's funny?' Paul asked. 'Some of the most important comedians in the world did outrageous things. Richard Pryor, Andy Kaufmann... '

'I always thought comedians were supposed to make people laugh,' Andy said. 'I haven't noticed anyone in my newsgroup laughing.'

'They're techies, they have no sense of humour,' Paul declared. 'Look, there's a guy meeting me here today, a fan of my flames, who wants to talk about starting a flame industry! And I'd be the leader of it. Do you know what this means? I could be famous! You're going to see me on the cover of *Rolling Stone*!'

'I don't think so, Paul,' Andy told him. 'Someone's coming to see you, but it's not a fan. It's some guys from the newsgroup who are planning to make you stop.'

'Yeah, right,' Paul snorted. 'Knock it off, Shaw, I don't believe you.'

Andy shrugged. 'It doesn't matter whether you believe me or not. They're coming. The guy who contacted you, the one who called himself MadDog? That's Twister, a subscriber to the Urban newsgroup.'

Paul said nothing, but Andy saw his eyelids flicker for a moment.

'Oh, Paul, this is really pathetic,' Andy said. 'Look, I know you like attention and you want to be funny. So learn some jokes, do something that makes people laugh! If nobody's laughing at you, that means you're not funny. You're just being obnoxious.'

'What do you know about comedy,' Paul muttered.

'Absolutely nothing,' Andy replied. 'I don't think you do either.'

Paul drummed his fingers on the table. He looked at the door again, but this time his expression was different. He's no Killer, Andy thought. Just a pitiful guy who wants attention and doesn't know how to get it in a better way. He couldn't hate Paul, he could only feel sorry for him.

'You don't have a lot of friends, do you, Paul?'

'Who needs friends?'

'You do. I do. Everyone does.'

'Gimme a break,' Paul sneered, but it came out sounding almost like a whimper.

'Just out of curiosity,' Andy said casually, 'how did you go on posting those flames after you were thrown out of the Double Click?'

'I got my own modem and an Internet provider.'

'Lucky you,' Andy said.

Paul shrugged.

'Surfing the Web a lot?'

'I don't know much about that,' Paul said, now watching the door nervously. 'All I know how to do is get into the newsgroups.'

'I saw a sign at the Double Click the other day,' Andy told him. 'They're starting weekly classes on how to use the Internet.'

'Doesn't do me much good,' Paul said. 'I'm not allowed in there, remember?'

'I'll bet if you talked to Greg, he might reconsider,' Andy said. 'If you told him you weren't going to fool around and interfere any more.'

The door to the restaurant opened. Three guys, all about their age, walked in and started looking around. Andy saw Paul tense visibly.

Andy looked at the guys and they looked at him. One of them came over to the booth.

'Twister?' Andy said.

'Yeah. Luke Malick.'

'I'm Andy513. Andy Shaw.' They shook hands. The other two guys came over, and Luke introduced them by their real names, James and Phil. Then they all looked at Paul.

Paul had gone white, and he seemed to be shrivelling up right before Andy's eyes.

Andy spoke quickly. 'This is Paul Reedy, he's in my class. I just ran into him.'

The guys nodded. 'Any sign of Killer?'

'No,' Andy said. 'I haven't seen anyone come in alone.'

'He's late,' Phil said, checking his watch.

'We're not in any hurry,' Luke said. He made a fist with one hand and smacked it against the palm of the other hand. 'Come on, let's get something to eat. We're going to need energy.'

'Boy, when I get my hands on that guy,' James was muttering as they headed towards a table.

Andy quickly reached in his pocket, pulled out his wallet, and tossed some money on the table. 'Come on,' he said to Paul. 'Let's get out of here.'

'Why did you do that?' Paul asked. 'Why did you save my butt?'

'I haven't the slightest idea,' Andy said. 'Maybe because I can't stand the sight of blood in a restaurant. Even the rare meat makes me sick.'

Paul grinned slightly. 'That's almost funny.'

Personally, Andy wasn't all that thrilled to get Paul's stamp of approval on his sense of humour.

Chapter Ten

Jessica was killing time at the Double Click, but it was getting harder and harder to do. She'd checked into the Girls Talk About Boys chat line, but today the usual nasty insults and the complaints weren't very interesting. She'd read just about every bit of information available on ice skaters and ice skating, and it only made her wish she was out on the ice right now, instead of being cooped up here, waiting to find out if her boyfriend was about to become her ex-boyfriend.

She saw that Blair was back at the bar again, so she went over. Blair barely acknowledged her. She was sipping furiously on a soda and staring into space.

A boy came over to her. 'Blair? I'm finished. I e-mailed it to you.'

'OK,' Blair said. 'I'll wait a few minutes, and check to see if it's there.'

He nodded. 'I'm going out for a walk. I'll be back in a little while.'

'Who was that?' Jessica asked Blair when he left.

'His name is Sean, he goes to Lakeside. He just took the Love Test.'

'Oh, yeah? He's cute. Whose questionnaire are you comparing his with?'

'Mine.'

'Oh. Hope this one works out better.'

'I had a ninety-six per cent agreement with Richie,' Blair said glumly. 'I doubt that any score Sean and I get could go higher than that.'

Jessica didn't know what to say to her. 'Well, good luck,' she said. Then added, 'Wish me luck, too.' Andy had just walked in.

He wasn't alone. That creep Paul Reedy was with him. Jessica watched as they both went to talk to Greg. As Andy left Paul there, he saw Jessica.

'Hi,' he said.

'Hi,' she replied. 'What are you doing with Paul? I thought he got thrown out of here.'

'He's trying to get Greg to let him back in. But he's sworn he's not going to pull any more pranks.'

'Do you believe him?'

Andy shrugged. 'I think you have to give people the benefit of the doubt. Maybe he really wants to change. Some people do.'

He looked at her directly. 'Some people can't.'

He's talking about himself, she thought. Or me. Or both of us.

'I need to check on something,' he said, and went to a computer station.

With a heavy heart, Jessica went back to her own. Had he read the advice from Chris1492 yet? Was he about to? Would it matter?

Her screen was still holding the image of an ice skater from a Web page. But then an Instant Message box appeared in the centre of the screen.

Andy513: *Are you there?*

Jess712: *Yes.*

Andy513: *Something is wrong with us.*

Jess712: *I know.*

Andy513: *I can't change myself for you.*

Jess712: *I don't want you to change.*

Andy513: *I don't want you to change either.*

Jess712: *You don't have to agree with me about everything.*

Andy513: *Neither do you. What are we going to do? Keep on arguing all the time?*

Jess712: *Maybe. We could start by talking.*

Andy513: *That's what we're doing.*

Jess712: *Not like this.*

Andy513: *IRL?*
Jess712: *Huh?*
Andy513: *In real life?*
Jess712: *Yes.*
Andy513: *When?*
Jess712: *Now.*

Blair looked at the questionnaire results on the screen. It looked like just a bunch of numbers. On its own, it had no meaning, it told her nothing. It had to be fed into the analysis program with her own questionnaire results, the one she'd completed for Richie.

It wouldn't take long, only a few minutes. Then she would know for sure. She could print out the results and show them to Sean when he returned. There it would be, in black and white. It would tell her that she could accept the date for tonight with no fear of taking an awful risk. Or it would tell her to say no, not tonight, not ever.

Tis better to have loved and lost
Than never to have loved at all.

Why couldn't she erase those stupid words from her mind? They were driving her crazy.

She looked around for a distraction. Just a few feet away from her, Andy and Jessica were speaking just loudly enough for her to make out their words.

'Then why did you listen to this Chris1492 if you didn't like his advice?' Jessica was asking him.

'Because I thought he knew something I didn't,' Andy said. 'How to be romantic. I guess I'm just not a romantic kind of guy.'

'That's OK,' Jessica said. 'I can deal with that. You know what? I'm not crazy about this Double Click Café. I mean, it's interesting once in a while, but I don't want to come here every day.'

'That's OK,' Andy said. 'We don't have to do everything together. Like...' He hesitated.

'What?' she prompted him.

'Like, I really hate ice-skating shows,' he said. 'I'm not kidding, Jess, I really get bored out of my mind at those things.'

'You don't want to take me to the big show next week? The one with the Olympic stars?'

'Not really,' he admitted.

She nodded. 'That's OK. I'll go with some friends from my skating class.'

'Great,' he said with relief. 'You know, I

just thought of something. I'll bet that Chris1492 picked his name from that stupid old rhyme we used to say to remember when Columbus discovered America.'

'You're probably right,' Jessica said. 'In fourteen hundred and ninety-two, Columbus sailed the ocean blue.'"

'Of course, Columbus didn't really discover America,' Andy remarked.

'It was the Vikings, right?'

'Not them either. You can't say America was 'discovered', it's not like it didn't already exist as a land. It was inhabited, people were already here. Native Americans, remember?'

'Sure, but Columbus – or Leif Erikson – or *somebody* found it, when no one in the Western World knew it existed.'

'But whoever it was didn't *discover* it,' Andy argued. 'Just because they didn't know it existed doesn't mean it didn't exist. It's like saying the Native Americans didn't exist.'

'Oh, you're just trying to be politically correct,' Jessica declared.

'There's nothing wrong with being politically correct,' Andy was saying when someone from a computer station hissed,

'Shut up and go outside if you want to talk!'

Blair watched them leave the café, and shook her head. There they were, still arguing over crazy things. Obviously, nothing at all had changed between them. They were still this completely weird misfit couple who were totally unsuited to each other. Their personalities were different, they didn't share any interests and they argued all the time.

So why were they together?

She knew the answer to that. Because they're in love. And whatever love was, for them it existed on a totally illogical plane. She would never understand this. But she wasn't sure she even wanted to.

She turned back to look at Sean's questionnaire on the computer screen again. Then, she placed her fingers on the keyboard.

It wasn't much later that Sean returned to the café. He came over to Blair's station and pulled over a chair so he could sit beside her.

'Did I give you enough time?' he asked. 'Are you finished?'

'Yes.' She forced herself to look directly into those liquid blue eyes, the eyes that had made her go limp the first time she met him. And there was the hollow feeling in her stomach…

'Have you made a decision?' he asked. 'I mean, has the computer made a decision?'

'I've made a decision,' Blair said. 'I'll go out with you tonight.'

She was rewarded with a glimpse of that glorious smile of his.

'So we matched up, huh?'

'Well, not exactly.'

'What do you mean?' he asked.

'I don't know if we match up or not. I didn't feed your questionnaire into the program. I never ran the comparison with mine.'

'What happened? Did the program break down?'

'No,' she said. 'Something broke down, but it wasn't the program.'

He looked puzzled. 'You're talking in riddles. What did you do with my Love Test?'

'I deleted it.'

'Why?'

'Because I don't want to know the results,' Blair told him. 'I'll take my chances.'

Oh, that smile. 'Let me see if I get this,' he said. 'You have no idea if we have anything in common, if we share any ideas or interests or anything, but you're willing to go out with me anyway?'

'That's right,' she said. 'I may end up regretting this, but—'

'You'll never know if you don't try,' he finished for her. 'Come on, I'll give you a ride home and you can change into your dancing shoes.'

'Uh, just a minute,' Blair said. 'Now, see, here's something the Love Test could have warned you about. I can't dance. I have absolutely no rhythm and I fall over my own two feet.'

'OK, how about this,' Sean said. 'I hate dancing.'

'You do?'

He nodded. 'See? We already have something in common.'

'If you hate dancing, why are you going to a school dance?' she asked him.

'Because it's a fund-raiser and I was on the committee that organised it,' he told her. 'Look, this will be great. While everyone else is dancing, we can spend our time taking the Love Test in person!'

As Sean opened the door, it almost hit a couple who were in a tight embrace against the wall.

'Uh-oh,' Blair said loudly. 'PDA.'

Jessica took her eyes off Andy just long enough to give Blair a 'get lost' look. Blair laughed.

'What's PDA?' Sean asked.

'Don't you have that rule at Lakeside? It's Public Display of Affection. We can get sent to detention if we're caught getting too close at school.'

'PDA,' Sean repeated. 'I'll have to remember that. I'm sure you've heard of CDA.'

'What's CDA?' Blair asked.

'Cyber Display of Affection. Getting too close online. Don't you think PDA sounds a lot more interesting?'

Blair just smiled. She was feeling very pleased to discover something else they had in common, too.

More love on the Net in

double·click·café:1

CYBER KISS

●

How can trendy, pretty Charlie, the most popular girl in the Junior year, have anything in common with the quiet loner Trent, the new kid in town? Come down to the Double Click Café and find out!

●

LIKE CYBERSPACE, THE DOUBLE CLICK CAFÉ IS FULL OF SURPRISES. YOU NEVER KNOW WHO YOU MIGHT MEET. YOU NEVER KNOW WHAT YOU MIGHT DISCOVER.